SUMMER OF THE BOMBERS

SUMMER OF THE BOMBERS

By
Jennifer Bohnhoff

THIN AIR BOOKS

cover designed by GetCovers
ISBN-13: 9798377066101

Names, places, characters and incidents depicted in this book are products of the author's imagination or are used fictitiously. Any resemblance to actual events, locales, organization, or persons, living or dead, is entirely coincidental and beyond the intent of the author.

Thin Air Books
P.O. Box 2 Sandia Park, NM 87047
jennifer.bohnhoff@gmail.com
www.jenniferbohnhoff.com

Acknowledgements

I am grateful to my critique buddies: Michele Hathaway, Susan Metallo, Diane Mittler, and Christine Ottaviano Shestak. All fabulous writers in their own right, they did a lot to make this story coherent.

Thanks also go out to my beta readers: Charon Leon, Heather Patrick, and especially to Eileen Wood, educator and horsewoman who catches the little things like no one else can.

I chose April 10, 2023 to publish this book because it would have been my father's 87th birthday. Jim Swedberg was enthusiastic about a lot of things including fly fishing, bicycle riding, backpacking, astronomy, and fossil and artifact hunting. An excellent writer, he passed away before my first book came out, but I know he would have been both proud and supportive. I miss you, Dad.

Chapter One
The Fire
April 22

"Wake up, Punkin." My Dad's voice pulled me from sleep. They were the words he always used, but his tone made my stomach clench. Something was wrong.

I opened me eyes. Orange, flickering light flowed in my window, backlighting my dad and making him look like a dark demon from one of those horror movies we watched every October.

The air roared outside, cracking and popping.

Nothing made sense.

"Wha?" I struggled up to my elbows.

"The fire, punkin. It's going to crest the hill. We've got to get out. Now."

The fire had been burning for three days. The Forest Service had started it, a simple, controlled burn to clear the forest floor of downed branches and pine needles. Better, they said, to do this in the spring when the ground was still damp with winter run off. All had gone well until the wind picked up and the fire got out of hand.

But what the Forest Service had started, the Forest Service could, and would, end. Before it threatened private property. TV newscasters, one hand to their ears, the other clutching microphones, had shouted that assurance all yesterday while smoke billowed behind them and bombers rumbled overhead. The bombers had bellies full of red slurry that would put out the fire. The newscasters had said so. The government had promised it.

Those bombers. They were everywhere that summer, buzzing like flies at a rodeo. The whole southwestern part of the United States seemed engulfed in flames. In my memory, that time will always be the summer of the bombers.

I squinted at my cell phone. Two fifty-three a.m. I shook my head to clear the haze. My mind flew through the checklists of things they'd said we needed to carry out if our house was in danger.

"The family pictures," I muttered.

Dad smiled. "We packed them last night, Punk. All the really important stuff. Your mom's finishing up now. Saddle up Wildfire. You're going to have to ride him out."

Hearing my bay's name got me out of bed. I threw off the quilt and raced around the room, stripping out of my sleep shirt and leaping into the first pair of tattered jeans I tripped over. I threw on the stretched out, dirty pink t-shirt I had been wearing when I mucked out the stables the day before, then pulled on my boots one at a time, hopping around the room to keep my balance.

It wasn't until I took off my boots two days later that I realized I hadn't put on socks.

My mother rushed around the living room throwing the contents of desk drawers and bookshelves into black plastic garbage bags. Shine, my little sister who's in second grade, wailed at her heels like she was a preschooler. Outside the back door, the Volvo's back hatch bulged with black plastic garbage bags. The air had the tang of Christmas, when all the neighbors had fires in their fireplaces. But it wasn't pleasant like it was at Christmas. This time it was so intense that it stung my eyes and burned my throat.

The hill behind our house looked like a hunched black beast. Angry orange and yellow clouds roiled up behind it. While I watched, the fire crested the hill. A tree exploded in a fireball. The yellow heat burned its shape into my eyeballs. I ran to the stable.

Wildfire danced in his stall, his eyes white-rimmed with terror. I climbed over the stall's wall, threw the blanket over him, then heaved the saddle atop it and cinched up the strap.

"Whoa, buddy, it's all right," I murmured, although I didn't believe myself. He champed and threw his head, but I slipped the bit into his mouth and climbed into the saddle before reaching down and slipping the bolt on the stall door.

Wildfire burst out, kicking and bucking like a rodeo bronco. I dropped the reins, and they danced loose on his neck. I didn't dare grab for them. It was all I could do just to hang on to the saddle horn. We careened out the stable door and skiddled past the Volvo, where dad was trying to slam the hatch. Bags ballooned out of the gap. I caught a glimpse of Shine's white face peering out the driver's window, her mouth open in a howl of terror. Dad's old beater of a pick-up truck, the one he used for runs to the dump and to bring home plywood sheets, was also piled high with bags and bundles.

Dad shouted something about me staying near my mother's car. I couldn't answer. Wildfire's sudden burst from the stables had knocked the wind out of me. The air was thick, like when my dad forgot to open the damper on the fireplace. It tasted sharp on my tongue, made my sinuses swell.

Dad lunged for the reins and Wildfire reared back. His front hooves slashed the air. He spun, kicking out with his back legs. Dad jerked back. Wildfire found the entrance to the driveway. His bucking turned into a full-blown gallop. As his gait smoothed out, I let go of the horn and reached for the reins, but no amount of tugging on them could convince Wildfire to slow down or rejoin the family. Instinct had told him that the road into town led away from the fire. I gave up trying to stop him, leaned low over the saddle horn, and let him decide where to go and how fast.

We weaved past cars bristling with chair legs and bulging with mattresses, their trunks stuffed so full that they couldn't be closed. They looked like Henry Fonda's car in *The Grapes of Wrath,* one of the old black and white movies my dad loved so much. Horns blared. People shouted. I thought of my family, stuck in the back of this mess, and I hoped the fire moved slower than the traffic jam. A fire truck and half a dozen police cruisers sped past on the dirt shoulder on their way up the hill. Why didn't one of the cruisers stop and sort this out? Wasn't that supposed to be their job?

It didn't take us more than fifteen minutes to get into town. Cars with tables and bicycles strapped to them clogged the streets. People milled about, shouting into their cell phones and at each other. I reached for my back pocket. It was empty. Had I left my phone on the nightstand, or had it fallen out during the wild ride? I rode about in circles wondering how long it would take for my parents to catch up with me. Where was I going to meet them when they got down the hill?

A big, army-green canvas tent sat on the edge of the gold course. Generators buzzed away, powering a rank of floodlights. Men and women rushed back and forth, shouting directions to each other. Some in heavy yellow outfits, kind of like what firemen wore, sat around on folding chairs drinking from Styrofoam cups. Some of them were soot smudged and slouched. Others – the clean ones -- sat upright. They looked jittery, their knees bobbing, keeping time with the roar of the generators, their hands flitting up to the helmets that sat back on their heads, the visors peering up at the sky. None spoke, but a few lifted cigarettes to their lips and sucked hard from time to time. Every once in a while, a bunch would jump up and rush off to climb into the backs of flatbed trucks.

At the center of the tent were folding tables piled with crates and radios, laptops and piles of papers. A man leaned over one table, his palms resting on either side of a map. He wore a rumpled forestry uniform and his face looked haggard in the glaring light. I figured he must be some sort of government official, someone who was supposed to help people like me. I slipped off Wildfire's back and led him toward the tent.

"Excuse me," I said, "I've lost my cell phone and I can't find my family."

He looked up, but his eyes didn't focus on me. "Check with the Red Cross." He looked back at the map. Behind him the radio kept up a high-pitched whine punctuated by bursts of unintelligible speech. Other men shouted directions.

"Where?"

He waved a hand vaguely, dismissively. I felt my breath catch in my throat and I thought for a moment that I might pass out or throw up. If this man wouldn't help me, who would? One of the smoke jumpers met my gaze. His face was black with grime, but his eyes were startlingly blue. "Do you know where the high school is?" he asked. The high pitch of the voice made me realize that he was a she.

I nodded. Since I was in the eighth grade, I'd be going there next fall.

"Check there. The Red Cross often sets up emergency shelters for evacuees in high schools."

Evacuees? The word reminded me of the people who had come last year after Hurricane Leonora devastated New Orleans. Big Army buses had brought them halfway across the country. They'd slept on army cots in the Alamitos High School gym for a couple of weeks before the government had found them places to stay. I remembered their disheveled, mismatched clothing and how their children clung to dirty dolls and broken, rejected toys donated from Goodwill. I wanted to tell this woman that I wasn't like those people. My family had a nice house, just a few miles out of town. And then I caught my reflection in her visor. I was dirty and disheveled, my pink t-shirt filthy from mucking out the stables yesterday, wrinkled from a night on the floor. I remembered the fire cresting the hill and realized that I might not have a home anymore. I nodded thanks because my throat was too dry and tight to speak, climbed on Wildfire's back, and headed for the high school.

Mattresses and chairs and dressers were piled on every car in the high school parking lot. One had a child's wading pool tied to its roof. I was staring at it when a lady in a khaki shirt and pants stepped out from between two cars. She clutched a clipboard to her chest and smiled up at me.

I pointed to the wading pool. "Those things cost almost nothing. They fall apart by the end of summer. Why would anyone save something like that?"

The lady shrugged. "People do irrational things when they're frightened. You an evacuee?" She held out a hand as if she intended to help me off Wildfire's back. I don't know why, but my stomach hardened. I stayed in the saddle and stared down at her.

"The fire might not reach my house," I said.

"Where are your parents?"

I jutted my chin towards the west, the direction I'd rode into town. "They're driving our car and truck down. We don't own a horse trailer, so I had to ride Wildfire out."

She nodded and made a notation on her clipboard. "Wildfire, you called him? Ironic name for a horse, considering. Your family's probably already inside getting registered. I'm Trudy Goodheart, of the Equine Assistance Agency. I'll take care of Wildfire for you while you go check." She offered me a business card. I gave it a quick glance before tucking it into my jean's back pocket.

She jerked her chin toward the far end of the parking lot where a four-horse trailer stood. "We've already got two other refugee horses. As soon as we're full I'll take them someplace safe. Just give me your name and phone number. And remember, you've got my card."

She held out her clipboard. It should have struck me as odd that the paper was just plain, white typing paper and not a form. Governments always use forms. Lots of forms. But I didn't know that, not yet. I handed Wildfire's lead over. He nuzzled the top of my head, then threw his head over my shoulder and drew me in close before Trudy led him into the trailer while I walked to the gym. I looked back once and saw the trailer parked there, the sky just beginning to turn pink with dawn behind it.

"Can I help you?" A woman with smudged glasses and a wild, uncombed tangle of gray hair looked up from the drifts of papers littering the folding table that blocked entrance into the high school gym. Her mouth split into the rigid, false smile that bus drivers and ticket takers give. The t-shirt stretched across her ample chest said "Volunteer." A big red cross undulated over her stomach.

The scene behind her looked like a giant slumber party. Kids ran between the army cots and piles of furniture, shrieking and laughing at their own games. Other kids thundered up and down the bleachers. Adults stood around, staring vacantly and clutching Styrofoam cups.

"I'm looking for my family."

"Name?" The woman looked down, shuffling through her papers before I even got a chance to answer.

"Davis," I said. "My father's name is Curtis. Mother's Elaine. I'm Margaret."

The woman shuffled her papers, her lips pursed into a pruney O. I shifted from foot to foot, searching the milling people for a glimpse of someone I knew.

"Punkin!" The sound of my dad's voice made me twirl around. As he walked through the door, he flashed a wide smile so big that even his bushy beard couldn't hide it. My mother and Shine, trudged along behind him. Mother's hair was disheveled, her clothes mussy, her eyes red-rimmed. Shine shuffled along in her footy pajamas. She clutched her faded, nearly hairless teddy bear to her chest.

"There you go! Found them." The volunteer beamed up at me self-importantly.

"Thank you," I said to be polite.

"Not at all," she answered, and went back to shuffling her papers. The fake smile looked like it had been permanently installed.

I turned back and saw the tension on my mother's face melt into sobs when her eyes locked on mine. She threw her arms around me. "I thought I'd never see you again," she said between sobs. "The crowds! The chaos! I thought you were gone forever." Shine wedged herself between us and began wailing. Dad wrapped his arms around the lot of us.

"It's okay now. We've got each other," he said, then disengaged himself from the group hug and moved to the lady at the table. When he'd gotten us registered, we moved through the gym until we found four cots to stake our claim on. Mom and Shine climbed onto two of them while Dad and I went back to the car to rescue Schrodinger, the family cat, who howled and scratched at his crate. After that, I wandered through the gym, searching for my friends and neighbors. I found the Andersons, who lived next door, and Mr. Chen, the elderly man who lived down the road from us. My friend Julia, who lived up at the end of our street, was there with her family, and we talked for a bit before I decided I'd better check back in with my mother. None of my in-town friends were there. I guessed they hadn't been evacuated.

"It's gone," Mother said as soon I sat down on my cot.

Shine sniffed and wiped her nose with the back of her hand. "All of it. My American Girl dolls. The dress up chest. Even Bilbo." Shine had won Bilbo the goldfish at the school carnival just last weekend. We still hadn't bought him a bowl, so he lived in an old pickle jar on the kitchen counter. Shine's face wrinkled up and she glared at our mother, who threw up her hands.

"There was so much to remember," Mom said.

I shook my head. "I saw a fire truck going up the hill. They spray the roof with water. That stops the fire."

"Not a fire that size," Mother said.

"What we need is cocoa!" Dad jumped to his feet and disappeared into the crowd.

"Wildfire's safe," I added. "A lady from the Equine Assistance League took him."

"While you were walking around, a lady came by and gave me this, to make me feel better. It's not working." Shine held up a plastic horse. I was willing to bet it came from the Goodwill. Tears spurted from her eyes. The white streaks on her black-smudged cheeks told me that this wasn't the first time she'd cried since she'd left home.

"We've lost everything," my mother said with a sigh.

I tried to sound upbeat. "Mother! It's only stuff."

My mother winced. "That's what your father said, too."

And just as she said it, dad came back and thrust a donut and a Styrofoam cup into my hand. "Have a donut. And some cocoa. They're free. I'm going to see what I can find out." He disappeared back into the crowd. I slumped onto an empty cot and ate. The gym smelled of smoke and sweat. Voices echoed through it. I didn't feel like roaming around like my father, but I didn't feel like sulking like my mother and sister either. I stretched out, and immediately fell into a deep, dreamless sleep.

When I look back it seems strange that I could sleep amid all that noise and uncertainty. At the time it was easy. I had found my family and secured a safe place for Wildfire. It seemed to me that the worst was over.

I wouldn't know how wrong I was until much later.

Chapter Two
The Morning After
April 23

The sound of a bomber woke me. The low rumble built, louder and louder, the pitch higher and higher until it roared overhead and faded into the distance. I stared at dust motes dancing in sunlight streaming through the high windows while I gathered my thoughts. At first, I didn't even remember where I was or why I was there. Like the sound of the bomber, my thoughts gathered until my head roared with them. I swung my legs over the cot's side bar. My body felt stiff, my brain sluggish, my thick and fuzzy tongue filled my mouth. A dull, throbbing headache droned behind my eyes, making it difficult to think.

I suddenly sucked in a breath, realizing that I was alone in the gym. My heart pounded. Where was everyone? I walked to the reception table, where a lady hunched over a paperback novel. She looked up. She wasn't the one who had "helped" me find my father.

"Good morning, Sunshine!"

Sunshine was my sister's nickname, not mine, but this lady wouldn't know that. My little sister was the sunshine in my family. She was blond, perky, little, and cute. I was Punkin, the chunky, redheaded, steady one. I was dependable and hardworking, but no one lit up when I came into the room. I wasn't anyone's sunshine.

"Where is everyone?" I asked.

"Off to breakfast. You must have been really tired to have slept through them all going. Feel better now? Here. Take this pass. Jack's Flapjack House'll let you eat anything on the menu. The Red Cross has a deal with them."

I squeezed my eyes shut, trying to force out the throbbing in my head. "What time is it?"

She picked her cellphone off the table and squinted at the screen.

"Oh, a little after ten."

Most kids my age sleep late, but not me. I'm up with the birds, mucking out Wildfire's stall at first light. I've got a restless spirit and it doesn't like to lie around. "Thanks. I've gotta go now. Gotta see about my horse and the house."

She raised her eyebrows. "You didn't leave your horse at home, did you?"

"No. Some lady from the Equine Assistance League took him last night."

"Equine Assistance League? You sure you don't mean the Humane Association of Santa Fe? They're the ones who are helping us with evacuee's pets."

I looked back at my family's cots. How come I hadn't noticed that Schrodinger's crate wasn't there anymore?

"Nope," I said. "A lady in the parking lot last night said she was from the Equine Assistance League and would take Wildfire someplace safe."

"Never heard of her, or the organization, but there's a lot of people assisting on this. I'll see what I can find out. Now, about your house: What street do you live on?"

"Ridgecrest," I said. Her face pinched into a mask of pity. It made me want to throw up the last remnants of donut. "Don't look at me like that. I haven't even given you the street address."

"I'm sorry," she said. "All of Ridgecrest is gone."

"You don't know that for sure." I spun on my heel and escaped into the sunlight before she could give me any more bad news. How could she know? It was all too new, too uncertain. Gossip floats around like ash during a forest fire, rumors and more rumors about how far the fire's reached, who's been burned out, who's been spared. I felt hollow, hungry and desperate to fill the emptiness with something.

The short walk from the high school to Jack's Flapjack House looked like the set for a movie about Armageddon. Roiling smoke clouds turned the sky into a bright yellow haze. Ash rained down like dirty gray snowflakes. People stumbled along, looking like sleepwalkers. Or zombies. They glanced towards the fire with jerky motions, as if they could not control their heads. I found myself glancing up, too, in a sort of nervous tic. I couldn't see the fire. No one could from here. But it was obvious that we all felt its presence. I heard it, too: not the fire itself, but the constant drone of the bombers coming over, their orange painted bellies full of water or that strange red slurry.

Dad waved his hand and leaped to his feet when I approached. He sat on one side of a booth with Mr. Chen, an older man who lived alone in a big house not far from ours. My mother and Shine sat on the other bench, their backs to me. I slipped in next to my mother. A waitress with a red name tag that had *Sheila* carved into it appeared with a menu. I waved it off and handed her my ticket.

"Seventeen," Shine said. I stared at her, confused. Was she ordering for me? But Shine just smiled as if she'd made a grand pronouncement, and the waitress was still looking at me expectantly.

"Two eggs over easy, hash browns and bacon," I said. "And a Danish and a big glass of orange juice."

Mom held out her hand to stop the waitress. "No you don't, young lady. You don't need all that."

"But it's free," I argued.

"It doesn't matter if it's free. You don't need to eat that much."

"Did you let Shine eat anything she wanted?"

Mom pointed to a glass dish in front of Shine. I could tell that it held the remnants of a yogurt, granola and fruit parfait.

I sighed. "How about hash browns and just one egg?"

"Eighteen," Shine said. I looked at her again. There was no number eighteen on the menu. What in the world was she counting?

Mom nodded and the waitress hustled away. In the silence that followed, I watched Mr. Chen open his napkin into a square, then fold the corners inward until they met in the middle. He folded the corners into the middle again and again, making the square increasingly smaller.

"How's my Punkin?" Dad asked.

"A lady at the gym said our house burned down," I answered. "But she can't know that for sure."

"They know." My mother dabbed her swollen eyes with a wadded-up napkin. She looked like she hadn't slept at all last night.

"Poor Bilbo," Shine said, then moaned as her eyes narrowed at Mother.

"We can get another goldfish. I mean, if we have to. I don't think we should trust the word of some lady sitting at a folding table in the gym," I said.

Shine leaned forward and shot me the same venomous glare she'd just given Mother. "Another goldfish won't replace Bilbo."

"Yeah. Right," I said with a snort. I could have lined up twenty jars with twenty goldfish and Sunshine wouldn't have been able to pick hers out. "At least we got Wildfire out. And Schrodinger. Where is he, anyway?"

"Didn't you hear when the Santa Fe Humane Association took all the pets this morning?" Dad asked. "I don't know which was louder, the dogs howling or their owners crying."

Shine shook her head. "Punk can sleep through anything."

"Cannot," I argued even though I knew my sister was right. A couple of years ago a tree came down in a big windstorm in the middle of the night. It crashed right through the roof but I didn't know anything about it until I got up for breakfast the next morning and found it lying across the kitchen table.

"Have you heard when FEMA's going to haul in the temporary housing?" Mr. Chen asked.

Shine cocked her head to one side. "What's FEMA?"

"The Federal Emergency Management Agency," Dad said. "We're going to have trailer homes just like the ones they used after Hurricane Leonora."

"Oh. Nineteen," Shine said.

My mother shuddered, clutching her coffee cup. "I really couldn't live in one of those."

"It's only temporary," Dad said. "Think of it as a little vacation home."

"Rebuilding may take years," Mr. Chen said. "Contractors are going to be hard to find. Every good builder in Northern New Mexico will be busy."

"I can do it myself." Dad took a long drink from his mug, then slapped it back down onto the table so hard that I jumped. "I've always wanted to build a house from the ground up!"

My mother stared at him, her jaw working but nothing coming out. My sister sniffled and moaned the name of her goldfish once again.

Dad shrugged. "Elaine, you've always hated the kitchen. I can build one just the way you want it. If you really can't live in FEMA temporary housing, we could shack up with Maureen and Dutch for a bit. You know they'd love time with the girls."

Mom shook her head. "My sister and her friend've done enough for me already. And I don't want to have to commute all the way from Albuquerque every day. I've got a job to go to, remember?"

"Don't make me miss the end of the year parties," Shine whined. I nodded. Starting at a new school this late in the year would be hard. My mother nodded and pointed her fork at Dad, who shrugged.

The waitress brought my plate. I smashed my egg with the back of my fork, mixed it in with the hash browns, then drowned the whole mess in ketchup. This was a treat. Dad never made hash browns and I loved them. "We aren't even sure it's gone," I said through a mouthful.

My mother's lower lip trembled. "I just can't believe the two of you! Neither of you have any sense of how great our loss is!"

"Twenty," Shine said.

I slammed my fork down on my place and glared at her. "You're giving me a headache. What are you counting, anyway?"

"The bombers," Shine said. "There've been twenty of them since we came in here."

I looked over at my dad, who seemed burning with excitement, then back at my mother, who was drowning in watery despair. They say opposites attract. That had always been true of my mother and father. My dad's the relaxed one. When I was born, he quit his job and stayed home because my mother earned more money than he did. My mother, on the other hand, took everything seriously, especially her top secret, really important job at the lab. My mother brought home the bacon. Dad cooked it. She kept a roof over our heads. He kept it from leaking. She made sure the bills were paid and checked my sister's and my homework. Dad made sure we knew that paying the bills and doing homework wasn't the only thing in life. They were different, but they worked well together. At least until now.

I shoveled in another mouthful of eggy hash browns, chewed quickly, then washed them down with orange juice. The faster I ate, the faster I could check on Wildfire and find out what was really going on with our house. "Okay," I spluttered through my last mouthful, "let's get back."

"You go ahead," Mr. Chen said. "I've got nothing to check on. Might as well read the paper and have another cup of coffee."

My family walked back through the dusky noon. Ash, some as big as dinner plates, drifted through the air, covering the ground in gray. Dad kept bringing up what he was going to do with the house, and Mom kept shushing him, and Shine kept whining about Bilbo, but I was too busy thinking about Wildfire to listen to any of them. When we walked into the gym, the lady at the folding table looked up. I could tell by the look on her face that she didn't have good news for me.

"Who did you say had your horse? The Horse what?"

"Equine Assistance League," I said.

"They met her in the parking lot," Dad added.

"Yes, there is." I reached into my back pocket and pulled out the business card the lady had given me. It said *Trudy Goodheart, Equine Assistance Agency.* There was a number and an address. I handed the card to the lady behind the desk, who frowned at it for a long time. Finally, she dialed the phone number on her cell phone. While she listened, she frowned some more. She hung up and dialed another number.

The lady shook her head. "You must have it wrong. There's no such organization."

"Hi Fred," she said, her voice brightening. "You on the computer? Good. I need you to do me a favor. Get on Google Maps. Find out what's at one-one-oh-six Cartland Boulevard."

"It's the Assistance Agency," I said, but the lady held up a hand, hushing me. There was a long pause.

"You sure?" she asked. "Well, okay. Thanks. Talk to you later." She hung up the phone and sat, biting her lip for what seemed like a long time.

"Well?" my mother said.

"The number on the card?" The lady said, "It's disconnected. And the address is the address for Jack's Flapjack House, where you just ate your breakfast. I'm afraid you've been the victim of a scam."

My hash browns and eggs threatened to come back up. Shine let out a wail, and my Dad said the kind of word he never says around us kids.

"Then where's my horse?" My question came out like a mouse squeak.

"I don't know," the lady said, punching numbers on her phone, "but I intend to find out."

Chapter Three
As Normal as Possible
April 24

"Wake up, Punkin." My dad's voice cut through the fog of sleep. My heart lurched. I jerked up, looking for flames. Was I trapped in a nightmare? A repeating a bad case of déjà vu? Or was I Bill Murray in my own version of *Groundhog's Day?*

None of the above. I was safe and secure on the cot in the high school gym.

Safe, yes.

Secure? Hardly.

"Ugh," I groaned, throwing myself back down. "What is it this time?"

"School," dad said.

I opened my eyes and stared at him. "You're kidding, right?"

Dad shook his head. "Nope. The social workers say it's best to keep you kids on a schedule. Make your life as normal as possible. And you'll see your friends."

"You think it's normal to wear this to school?" I grabbed the front of my filthy pink t-shirt. I had worn it to muck out the stables the day before the fire. Wearing it day and night for three days hadn't made it any cleaner. "The way I smell, my friends won't get within ten feet of me!"

"I'm sure they'll understand. And I'm sure you won't be the only one who's been affected by this fire."

I groaned, but sat up and put my feet on the floor. "I won't be able to concentrate in class. I'm going to sit there and wonder what's going on in the search for Wildfire."

"Sitting and stewing about it isn't going to help anyone find your horse. The proper authorities have been notified. We have to give them time to do their work. Going to school is better than sitting around here all day doing nothing. You and me, we've never been good at just sitting around with nothing to do. So, get up and throw some water on your face."

I tilted my head, thinking. "So, is Shine going to school in her footie pajamas?"

Dad grinned. "She was super excited about it! She's going to be the center of attention!"

"OK," I said, and sighed deeply. "And you, Mr. Eager Beaver? What are you going to do?"

"I'm going to see what I can do about getting everyone a change of clothing and some toiletries. You're going to feel a lot better once you've had a shower tonight and gotten into some clean clothes."

I snorted. "You're right about that! And my phone? Can you try and get a replacement?"

"I'll see what I can do. I promise to check in at the sheriff's office about Wildfire, too. You and Shine'll get breakfast and lunch at school today. Your mother's going to work. She's already talked with Larry, that co-worker of hers. He says the big brass says that the Labs are safe from fire and the work needs to continue. Let's all do the best we can at what we can, ok?" Dad gave me a little hug, then slapped my butt to get me moving. I walked the half mile to Alamitos Middle School, crossing athletic fields that were sprinkled with ash. The wind must have shifted overnight, because the air didn't smell nearly as smoky, and no new ash drifted down. I walked backwards over the soccer field so that I could study the roiling black column that rose from behind the closest mountain. It spread into an ominous, black thunderhead that looked kind of like the mushroom cloud of an atomic bomb explosion. A tiny plane, a speck of white with an orange belly, passed in front of the blackness. Even though the fire looked far away, I still didn't feel safe.

Would I ever feel safe again? How long before life really got back to normal instead of me pretending that it was? How long before I had clean clothes to wear, and dad had a kitchen to cook in? How long before we had a home again? How long before Wildfire was home? If they found him before we rebuilt the barn, where would I keep him? A million questions whirled around, like ash through the air. I felt like my head was on fire.

Everyone in the cafeteria froze when I walked in. Only the kids who got free lunches and breakfasts ate here before school. They all knew each other, and they knew that I'm not one of them. Or, at least I wasn't until the fire. Now, I was homeless and filthy and probably looked like an extra in *Night of the Living Dead.* I stared right back, unsure what to say or do. Finally, a guy named Gabe, who's in my social studies class, unfroze enough to smile and wave.

"Grab a burrito and sit with us!" he said, and I did it, even though I didn't know anyone else at the table.

We aren't allowed to wear torn jeans to school. On my way to first period, several teachers gave my exposed thighs the eye, but when they looked up and saw who was wearing them, they looked the other way. Apparently, when you've been through hell and back, administration lets you wear whatever you want. Not that I wanted to wear these jeans anymore. I've been in them for days.

Martina Maldonado and Tiffany Huffstutler, my two best rodeo buddies, were standing near our lockers. They stared at me, open mouthed and as frozen as the breakfast crowd had been, then they shook themselves awake and hugged me in spite of my smell. I fought back tears, grateful to finally have someone acknowledge me.

"EEEEE! We've been so scared for you. I've texted you, like, a bazillion times and you never answer," Martina said.

"I couldn't. Lost my phone," I said.

Tiffany's face contorted in horror. "In the fire?"

"Or on the ride into town. I'm not sure which," I answered. "Everything happened so fast."

"No phone! That's really rough," Tiffany said, as if losing the phone is worse than losing the house and all my belongings.

"You'll have to tell us all about it," Martina said. "At lunch?"

I nodded, and we went our separate ways. All morning long, teachers and fellow students alike lavished pity on me. No one asked me about my house, or why my clothes were wrinkled and smelly, but I heard them whispering behind my back and I saw the pity in their eyes. They knew.

At lunch, I grabbed my tray and made my way to my usual place.

"Gawd," Tiffany said, gawking at my lunch tray. "She gave you even more pizza than she gives the football players."

"I think she's feeling sorry for me," I muttered, picking the pepperonis off the top piece in the stack. Half of my stomach wanted to eat all four of the pieces that the lunch lady piled on my plate. The other half roiled like that column of black smoke I saw on the walk to school.

"How's Julia? She lived up at the end of your street, right? She wasn't in math with me this morning," Martina said.

I nodded and stuffed in a piece of pepperoni. "She's got a grandma in Santa Fe. She'll be going to school there for the rest of the year. "

"¡Que trágica!" Martina said. "She's going to miss eighth grade graduation."

I wanted to say that missing a stupid ceremony is the least of her worries. Julia's dog, Pequeño, broke free when they were trying to wrestle him into the car, and they still haven't found him. She's going to miss her life, period. But would Martina and Tiffany understand when they haven't lived through the inferno that Julia and I have? I doubted it.

"So, you and Wildfire want a ride to the Socorro rodeo this weekend? Dad's saving the second stall in the trailer for you." Martina's eyes shone with excitement. She and I vied for best pole bender in the state, while Tiffany and I tried to beat each other at goat tying. Now, I guessed, the contests were over.

"I can't," I said. "Don't have Wildfire."

Martina and Tiffany's faces fell. "He didn't . . . didn't die, did he? In the fire?" Tiffany asked in a quavering voice.

I shook my head. "I rode him out. But somebody stole him once I got to town."

Martina groaned. "That's awful. No horse. No phone. Your life has really been turned upside down."

"Know what else I miss? My buckle." I pointed to the table, but both Martina and Tiffany know what I'm talking about. I watched their hands instinctively go to their own buckles, and knew they understand how important it was to me. They started talking about their horses, Pancho and Spunky Jean, and how they couldn't live without them. Maybe they were trying to be sympathetic, but talking about what you have when someone else has nothing doesn't help. Then they returned to talking about the rodeo that weekend, and how they were preparing for it. I felt like I was shrinking into the distance, as tiny and ineffectual as that bomber against the black smoke column.

The bell rang. Martina put a hand on my arm. "Tell us what we can do to help, ok? We want to. Both of us do, but we don't know what you need."

"How 'bout you turn back time?" I asked. Too late, I realized how sharp my voice had been. Sharp enough to be cutting. I nodded and pushed away from the table, happy to escape. I went to gym class, where I found that I did have a second set of clothes: my gym clothes. Since they were cleaner than my t-shirt and torn jeans, I wore them the rest of the day: another dress code infraction that administration ignored.

When I walked back into the high school gym at the end of the day, the front lobby was filled with people standing in lines. Folding tables had become portable offices for insurance agents and distribution centers for charities and businesses that were trying to help out. One line was for government vouchers to get towels and changes of clothing at the Wal-Mart. An airline company handed out travel kits filled with toothpaste and toothbrushes, combs and razor blades. Next to a Holiday Inn banner, a lady gave away little bottles of shampoo and soap. I searched the crowd for my dad. The lady at the front table waved at me.

"Did you find out who has my horse?" I asked when I made it over to her table.

She shook her head. "I didn't. What I was able to discover was that three other people fell for the same scam. I've got people working on it. Your father's talking with one of them right now." She gestured to a far corner of the lobby, where I saw my dad huddled on a folding chair, talking to a man in an overstuffed white shirt. I joined them, and we went over what I remembered about Trudy Goodheart and her Equine Assistance Agency.

Afterwards, I finally got to take a shower in the gym's locker room. I stood under the warm stream for a really long time, soaping up over and over and watching the water running down the drain become clearer and clearer. Then I changed into the fresh new clothes that dad got for me. He'd managed to get the right sizes for everything, even my bra and sneakers. I guessed that my mother had given him a list.

A little after sundown, volunteers from the First Baptist Church fed us barbequed brisket, beans, and coleslaw, scooping the food out of big aluminum pans and plopping it onto Styrofoam plates. They added a healthy dose of pity to the food as they served it. I remembered treating the hurricane refugees the same way, and it gave me a strange mixture of anger and shame. I vowed I would never give people who were in trouble 'that look' ever again. They – and we – may be down, but we still have our dignity.

Throughout dinner, the drone of bombers throbbed in the background, making my head throb. But at least Shine had stopped counting them.

Chapter Four
Only Temporary
April 25-May 7

Three days after the fire, they let us go see the house. Rather, they let us see the ash-strewn concrete pad that used to be our house. My heart, which had been hopeful until then, felt like it shriveled into a little raisin of a heart when I saw all that remained of our house: a few pipes that poked out where the bathroom had been and, strangely, the fridge and dishwasher, their paint blistered and peeled. Mother opened the dishwasher door and found four place settings of grandma's china, a few cups and glasses, a handful of silverware, and one pot.

Nothing else remained of either the house or the barn. No Bilbo in a pickle jar on the kitchen counter. No pickle jar. No kitchen counter. Shine poked through the ash with a warped piece of rebar while my mother and dad packed the contents of the dishwasher into a box.

The ground radiated heat into my new, pristine-white sneakers as I walked the perimeter of where our house used to stand. I kicked through the ash where my bedroom used to be, hoping to find the belt buckle I won at last year's rodeo finals. Surely something that big and solid couldn't have disappeared? My tears left clean circles on the concrete pad. The grand ponderosas which had towered over our house looked like black telephone poles. I averted my eyes from their ugliness. Bile burned my throat.

"Anything you want," my dad said when we were back in the Volvo and heading toward town. "That big bay window you've yearned for. The island in the kitchen. I can put them in for you."

My mother turned her face to dad. Her cheeks were wet. "Can you remake Grandma's rocker? The cedar chest that came over from Denmark with my great grandfather?"

"Aw, hon. Be realistic." It was a strange comment coming from my dad. My mother turned her head and stared out the window. The only sound remaining in the car was my sister's hiccupping sniffles.

"Hey," Martina Maldonado said as I set down my tray across from her and Tiffany a few days later. "What's up?"

"Nothing," I said. "Absolutely nothing."

Tiffany's bottom lip stuck out. "It's been a week. You're still sleeping in the gym?"

I nodded. "The ones whose houses didn't burn went home long ago. Others have gone to motels, or, like Julia, went to live with relatives. But not my mom and dad. Our closest relatives are in Albuquerque, and Mom says she has to stay here and work. So, we're waiting for the government to haul in the temporary housing they promised us."

"That sucks," Martina said. "How about Wildfire? Any word?"

I shook my head. "I've talked with agents from the insurance company and the sheriff's office and the FBI. No one has a clue where Wildfire is or how to get him. They all keep telling me to be patient, that something will turn up."

"Have you talked with my cousin yet? The one I told you about?"

I didn't answer Martina's question. My mind wandered. Some of the officials I've talked with were sympathetic, their limpid eyes bleary with apology. Others seemed gruff and uncaring. But all wanted me and my dad to fill out forms. Lots and lots of forms. I wondered where all those forms had gone. Probably into file cabinets, never to see the light of day again.

"I don't think I could be patient if it was my horse that was missing," Martina said. I glared at her. Was she suggesting that she loves her horse more than I love Wildfire? She must have seen the question in my eyes, because she looked down at her plate, stirring the mashed potatoes with her spork. "Is there something we can do? Put up posters at the rodeo this weekend?"

"I'm not going to the rodeo," I said.

"We could do it for you." The look on Martina's face reminds me of the pitying look on some of those social workers' faces.

"I don't need charity," I snapped.

"When are you going to start rebuilding your house?" Tiffany asked. I could tell she was anxious to get me off Martina's back, find something that I could be happy to talk about.

"Not anytime soon," I responded. "Dad can't just start banging together two by fours. And there aren't any building supplies available, since everyone's rebuilding at the same time. Besides, we can't afford supplies until the insurance company gives us money. And, we don't even have a building plan or the proper permits yet."

"Oh." Tiffany squirmed and looked at Martina, who was still stirring her potatoes. We ate in silence as I thought about how my family needed to replace so much. Our clothes. Our furniture. School supplies. Books. Pots and pans. Silverware. The debit cards from FEMA, the federal agency that was supposed to be helping us, had paid for a few changes of clothes and some toiletries, but not anywhere near enough to replace what'd been destroyed.

When I got back to the gym after school, Dad was talking with a man in a three-piece suit. Shine slouched on the floor at his feet. She looked like she was just about to burst into tears. "Hey Punk! We're moving! Into a new house!" Dad said.

"Not the old house. Not OUR house," Shine said. I knelt down and tried to explain to Shine that this was only temporary. The man pulled about two dozen papers out of his briefcase. Dad signed them all.

"There ya go, Mr. Davis. Compliments of the U.S. government. Remember to vote this fall." The man handed over a map and a key, then got up and moved to the next set of cots, where he'd go through the same process.

Dad smiled at me. "Now that we've got our own house, let's drive down to Santa Fe and rescue Schrodinger from the animal shelter."

Shine let up a wail. "I don't want to! I been sitting at a desk all day long! I want to go play!"

I rolled my eyes. "I can stay here and watch Shine," I muttered.

"Or I can. I could use a bit of fresh air." Mr. Chen, the elderly man who lived down the road from us when we all still had houses, left his cot in the corner and was absently batting the side of his leg with a rolled-up newspaper. "Really. I'm in no rush to go see the new house FEMA's given me. I can sit in the park and read my newspaper while Shine plays on the jungle gym."

Dad stroked his beard. "You sure, Carl?"

"Sure. It'll be no problem at all." Mr. Chen held out his hand and Shine jumped to her feet and followed him outside. Dad and I climbed into his old pick-up truck. We drove down to Santa Fe to spring Schrodinger, who howled all the way home.

"No question whether Shrodinger's alive or dead in that box," Dad shouted over the howling. "Why don't you text Mom and tell her we're on our way back up the hill."

"Can't." I shouted back. "You haven't replaced my phone yet."

Dad chuckled and fished his phone out of his back pocket. I texted Dad's message to my mother and gave her the address. She texted back that she could pick up Shine and still beat us there. When we got to town, we turned into what used to be an empty meadow but was now filled with row upon row of little white mobile homes. Not the kind that actually look like homes. These looked like the portable classrooms at school. They were all up on concrete posts, all had identical, white, metal sides. White Venetian blinds in the windows. Rust-red metal stairs leading up to rust-red metal doors. A neighborhood of Stepford houses.

The edges of the new, sticky black asphalt road were frayed and crumbling, with weeds sticking out here and there as if the road was already deteriorating. Even though Dad drove really slowly, the road came to pieces under the wheels, throwing a pitter patter of gravel onto the underside of the truck. We passed a postage-stamp sized park: a bench and a jungle gym on a patch of bare dirt. Kids with grimy faces swarmed over the jungle gym while a tired-looking mother slumped on the bench.

I peered at the piece of paper my dad clutched in his right fist. The map, xeroxed so many times that it looked sketchy, the lines fading into rows of dots, showed little rows of boxes. One box was circled in red. "Number one-oh-five," Dad read off the map through teeth that clenched the key to our new trailer house. We pulled up right behind my mother's car, in front of a house whose door was stenciled with 105 in drippy-looking white paint. Dad turned off the engine. In the silence I heard children screeching and laughing far away in the distance. I didn't feel like laughing. The screech that welled up in my gut was one of horror. Did the government really think that this little white box could replace my home? The stench of fresh asphalt and paint mades me want to vomit.

My mother slammed the door of her car and marched over to my Dad's open window. "I can't believe you left Shine with a stranger."

"Mr. Chen's not a stranger. We've known him since we moved onto Ridgecrest," Dad answered. Mom glared at him, then shifted her glare to the house. "That's it?"

"Looks like something from *Stallag 17*," I muttered.

"No, it doesn't. The POW barracks in *Stallag 17* were wooden. Besides, it's only temporary," Dad answered. "Until we rebuild."

Sunshine opened the Volvo's back door and threw herself out. "I get first dibs on a bedroom!" she shouted, bounding up the stairs to the front door. The stairs clattered. No one was ever going to be able to sneak up on us here. Shine rattled the front door knob, then turned and pouted at the three of us. My mother sighed. She reached in the open window and ripped the keys from Dad's mouth. My sister erupted through the finally-opened door with a squeal of delight. My mother followed her in.

Dad turned and smiled at me, a tight, nervous smile. "Well, Punkin? Shall we join them?" I muttered a halfhearted assent and schlepped Schrodinger through the front door, where I found my sister standing in the middle of the room, her fists clenched and her pretty face screwed up and red.

"What?" I asked.

"There's only two bedrooms," Shine wailed.

"So?"

"It's not fair. I'm tired of sleeping with other people!""

"Life's not fair," Mother said.

"Besides, it's only temporary. Until we rebuild," Dad said as he came through the door. He set down a cardboard box of canned goods that FEMA has given us and looked around, scratching his beard. I looked around, too. The public part of the house had only one big room, which served as living, dining and kitchen. The whole floor was covered with the kind of white linoleum that reminded me of hospitals and clinics. The walls were white. The blinds were white. The beige upholstered furniture looked cheap and plain. In the corner was a cabinet with a tiny sink, a refrigerator not much bigger than I was, a little gas range, and a dinette set that had metal and vinyl chairs and a formica-covered table. Two doors lead into two tiny bedrooms, which shared a bathroom the size of the ones on an airplane. The bedroom which my sister and I would share had two metal-framed beds, one against each wall. One tiny dresser stood between them.

"Good thing we don't have a lot of clothes," I said, setting my sister into a wail of protest.

"Punk! Stop badgering your sister," my mother shouted. I reached out and pulled Shine to me, shushing her. This place was going to be sheer hell if someone couldn't keep the peace among us. I thought that someone was me, whether or not I liked it.

"It's only temporary, until we rebuild," Dad said again. I wished I knew how long that would take. This situation couldn't end soon enough.

Chapter Five
A Little Help
May 20-27

I slammed my lunch tray onto the table. Martina Maldonado and Tiffany Huffstutler both jerked in surprise.

"I take it things aren't going well," Tiffany said.

"I am so tired of everything being temporary. It's an excuse for everything being whacked out, when nobody wants to take responsibility for it," I said.

Tiffany and Martina looked at each other. Something passed between them. Have they been talking about me behind my back? "Such as?" Martina asked.

"Such as, the oven's so small Dad can't bake cookies, but he says it's only temporary until we can rebuild. And Shine's bed squeaks! Every time she rolls over! But Dad's not going to bother fixing it because it's only temporary until guess when?"

"Until you rebuild," Tiffany and Martina said in chorus.

I was on the edge of hyperventilating and I felt my fingernails digging into my palms. I'd thought it would be good to get this off my chest, but I was wrong. The more I talked about it, the more agitated I felt. I nodded and took a deep breath so I could continue anyway. "And there's a crack between the walls and the floor in my bedroom. A breeze blows through at night, bringing in a lot of dust. But it's only temporary. It wouldn't be so bad if we had some kind of timeline, but we don't. We may have to live like this forever."

Martina's eyebrows shot up. "Don't you think forever's a bit of an exaggeration?"

"The city planners are too busy getting sewer and streets and electric lines back up to approve building permits. It's beginning to look more and more like we aren't going to rebuild for at least a year. Maybe even two. That feels like forever to me. I'm tired of waiting for somebody to do something!"

Tiffany and Martina looked at each other again. It looked like Tiffany had lost a bet or something. She swallowed hard. "Martina and I have been thinking. Yeah, you're in a bad situation. But, what if you did something about it?"

"Like what?" I threw my hands up in exasperation.

"Like buy some smaller cookie sheets and make the cookies yourself."

"Or try some WD-40 on Shine's bedsprings. And use a hammer and some nails on that gap in the wall," Martina added. They both looked at me and nodded. I leaned back and stared at the ceiling.

"Like I've got money for cookie sheets! And hammers and nails! And WD-40!"

"We can loan you stuff," Tiffany says. "Dad's got WD-40 in the garage."

"And we can come over and help nail that wall down," Martina said.

I sucked in a breath. I knew what my two friends were trying to do. They're trying to get me off my butt. They wanted me to fix my problems. But I'm not the one who caused them. I didn't burn down the forest. I didn't steal my horse. And now I had two supposed friends nagging me on top of everything else. I glared at them. "Fine. Okay. I've got a gift card that I'm supposed to use to buy summer clothes, but I haven't yet. So I'll buy some stuff and I'll make some cookies. AND I'll fix the squeaky bed. AND the gap. But it's not going to help." I pushed my tray away and stormed out the cafeteria. Some friends I had.

When I got back to the white tin can we're supposed to call home, I was clutching a plastic shopping bag from the grocery store in my fist. Shine sat at the table, her tongue sticking out of the side of her mouth as she worked on math problems. Dad was half buried in a nest of blankets he's made for himself on the sofa. "Hey, Punk. What'cha got there?"

I glared at him for a moment. He didn't even look guilty that I was the one doing something to help us get back to normal. "Tiffany and Martina suggested I try and fix some of the things that need fixing around here, so I got some supplies. I'm going to try to make this place a little more livable, even if it's just temporary. I need your help."

"Sure thing, Punk." Dad answered without turning around. He was watching *General Hospital,* or some other silly soap opera. He said it was good to see people whose lives were even more messed up than ours. I thought it was just an excuse for him to stare at nothing in particular, something he'd been doing a lot lately. I watched him a moment, waiting for him to get off the sofa. He didn't. I turned the bag over and dumped the contents on the kitchen counter. Loudly.

Shine looked over. Her tongue rolled along her top lip. "Cookie dough," she said.

"Yep. And I bought this little tray to bake them on. It's made for toaster ovens, but it'll do for us." I set the oven temperature according to the directions on the tube of cookie dough, then sliced the dough into rounds. "Hey Dad, if I put the dough in and set the timer, will you take the cookies out when the timer bings?"

"Sure thing, Punk." Dad said again. I stared at him a moment, then decided to take him at his word. When the oven came up to temperature, I slid the toaster oven tray in and set the timer. I grabbed the can of WD-40 and headed for the bedroom, where I flipped Shine's mattress up so it stood against the wall. I squirted WD-40 on each of the metal springs, then dropped the mattress back on top and sat on it. It still squeaked, although not as much. I flipped the mattress back up again, determined to destroy the squeak.

Beep, beep, beep. The timer went off. So did Shine. "Punk? The cookies are ready!"

"Dad?" I called, "You gonna get those?"

Beep, beep, beep.

"Dad? The cookies!" I squirted a couple more springs, then threw the mattress down again. It still squeaked.

Beep, beep, beep.

"They're burning!" Shine shrieked.

I dropped the can of WD-40 and raced out the door. The cookies were definitely not burned, but they were browner than I liked them. Defeat rolled over me. I'd failed to make anything better. Tears gathered in the corner of my eyes.

"You ruined them!" Shine's shout pulled me out of my defeat. I put up a hand, stopping her like a traffic cop stops oncoming traffic. I was definitely not the one who ruined the cookies. I glared at dad, who continued to stare at the TV. One at a time, I jabbed the cheap dollar store spatula under each cookie, scraping it off the sheet and sliding it onto a plate because we still didn't have a cooling rack. With each jab of the spatula, I told myself that I was right, that nothing was getting any better. I couldn't wait to give Tiffany and Martina a piece of my mind.

I stuffed a cookie into my mouth, burning my tongue. The sweetness told me that I was wrong. A cookie, even a slightly burned one, was better than no cookie at all. I was making a difference. I picked up the hammer and the little plastic container of nails I got in the housewares aisle. "I'm going outside."

"Aren't you going to make more cookies?" Shine asked.

"Not until I can be here to pull them from the oven when the timer goes off. I can't trust anyone around here to help." I glared at dad some more. He didn't even notice. I stomped out the door and around to the side, where the wall has bowed away from the floor. I thought of Shine and whammed in the first nail. At first, it didn't budge, but a second hit and the head buried itself. I was sure it'd gone high and was poking up out of the corner in my room, but it'd be under the beds or behind the dresser so it wouldn't hurt anyone and no one would notice. I thought of Dad when I hammered in the next one, which also went in too quickly. I reached my hand under the floor and felt it sticking out beneath. Too low, but what does that matter? I thought of Trudy Goodheart as I whammed away on the next nail. It went in perfectly. Not too high, not too low. I felt a little more powerful, a little more in control as I whammed in the next nail, thinking of one of those stuffed-shirt bureaucrats who cared more about getting out the vote than helping us get back on our feet. I thought about the friends who've deserted me and the volunteers who were puffed up with their own importance. I thought about the sheriff deputy assigned to find Wildfire. The nail went in with a single wham.

I was more relaxed when I stepped back into our tin can house than I had been in ages. Dad was still staring at the TV. I turned away, unwilling to argue with him. Shine had licked clean the tube of cookie dough. Although I wanted to shriek *I hope you get salmonella*, I turned away from that, too. Five overcooked cookies and a wall that no longer bulges may not be much, but it was a start.

I marched to where our lockers were the next morning and found Tiffany and Martina already there. They both turned at the same time and looked at me.

"You look different," Martina said. "More like your old Spunky Punky self."

"I took your advice yesterday," I confessed. "The cookies were awful, and the bedsprings not much better. But the hole between the wall and floor is gone."

Tiffany and Martina both broke into big smiles. Tiffany pumped her fist in the air. "Next stop, world domination."

I shook my head. "Next stop, the Sherriff's office. There's a deputy assigned to the missing horses. I think he needs a little prodding."

Martina's forehead wrinkled. "Which deputy? I might be able to provide you some ammo."

When I marched into the Sherriff's office on my way home from school, a man I assumed was the receptionist looked up from the front desk. "May I help you?"

I nodded. "I'm looking for Ernesto Chavez. Is he in?"

The man frowned. "Do you have an appointment?"

I placed my hands on the counter and leaned forward. "Isn't he the deputy in charge of investigating Trudy Goodheart and her Equine Assistance Agency? The one that stole four horses during the recent wildfire?"

"Well, yes." The receptionist looked a little hot under the collar. Funny, that an eighth-grade girl could yield such power.

"My horse was one of the ones stolen."

The receptionist's eyes darted to the right, towards a door with a frosted glass panel. I didn't ask. I walked over and opened the door.

The deputy was leaning back in his chair, his cowboy boots on the desk and his face buried beneath a black Stetson and behind his phone. "What is it?"

I pulled the door closed behind me. "Are you Ernesto Chavez?

Deputy Ernesto Chavez?"

He looked up, a scowl on a face that would have been handsome if it wasn't so angry. "And you are?"

"The Deputy Ernesto Chavez who's supposed to be in charge of investigating Trudy Goodheart and her Equine Assistance Agency? And who is Martina Maldonado's cousin?"

The scowl on his face grew even harsher. "And you are?"

"Margaret Davis. I'm the owner of Wildfire, one of the horses that Trudy Goodheart stole." I stuck out my hand over the top of the desk. Deputy Chavez didn't shake it.

"Allegedly stole," he muttered.

"Stole," I said emphatically. "I was there. I know what happened. I'm also your cousin Martina's best friend, and she suggested I come see you. She and I want to know what you've done about it so far. She says I should report directly to your abuela if you're not doing your job."

The frown on Deputy Chavez's face turned into a grin. He put down his phone, swung his feet off the desk, and sat up. "Now, that's what I call pulling rank! Sit down and I'll share with you what little I know."

Deputy Chavez didn't know much. He'd checked in with other Sherriff's offices, but no one had any leads. Just knowing that he was looking made me feel better, though.

Two evenings later, I was sitting next to Shine at the dinette set, trying to simultaneously write a last-minute essay and help her with two-digit addition when my mother walked in the door.

"Look at you!" she said.

"What?" Dad's face turned towards my mother, though his bleary eyes don't seem to focus on her. He reached up and scratched under his beard, which had grown shaggy.

"It was bad enough when you were watching *Days of Our Lives* and *General Hospital.* But this? You don't even speak Spanish!"

"So?" Dad asked.

"So, why waste your time watching a show you can't even understand?"

Dad shrugged. "Seems I don't understand much these days. Besides, time, I have a lot of."

"Then, why can't you find the time to fold these?" Mom picked a sock off a pile of clean laundry that sat on the sofa next to dad. She brandished it threateningly, then slam-dunked it back onto the pile.

Dad's eyes sharpened. His jaw clenched. "I'll get around to it."

"And dinner? Think you'll get around to making dinner sometime before midnight?" My mother's voice had risen to a shriek.

My heart pounding, I grabbed Shine's hand and pulled her into our bedroom. I'd never heard my parents fight before. Sure, they disagreed on occasion. Sometimes they even bickered. But I'd never heard my mother shriek at my dad. Not even that time last summer when we'd been so busy with a craft project that he'd gotten nothing else done all day long.

Dad's voice came out in a bellow. "Your life has gone back to normal! You still have a job to go to! A schedule to keep! That Larry guy to work with. Go to lunch with. Meet after work for a drink. Me? I got nothing! No home to build. Nothing to fix. I'm stuck all day in this white tin box, waiting for life to start again, waiting to be in control of something! Anything! And you don't care!"

"You think it's easy for me?" my mother shrieked back. "I work hard all day, and come home to this?" Something hit the wall, which rattled so hard that the lamp fell off the nightstand that sat between our beds. Shine began to cry.

"Come on, Shine. Let's go for a walk and give them some privacy." I popped the screen out of the window and climbed out. Hand in hand, we walked down to the postage stamp park, where we climbed to the top of the jungle gym and tried to catch a breath of fresh air. Even from here, we could hear our parents shouting. Some things I could help fix.

But not everything.

Chapter Six
Running Away from it All
July 15

I opened the door on the teeny-tiny refrigerator in our white, tin can house and stared inside it for a long time, trying to decide what I could throw together for dinner tonight. I'd been making dinner a lot lately, trying to keep my parents from arguing or me and Shine from starving.

"How about tuna helper?" I asked, pulling a box of dinner mix and two cans of tuna from the box of groceries that sat by the counter. No one answered. I glanced over at the pile of laundry on the sofa. Dad, or at least Dad's body, was buried in it somewhere. I didn't know where his mind had gone to. I was not sure if this change in him was temporary anymore, either. Without something to do, some purpose to keep himself busy, he'd lapsed into a lethargy so deep, I wasn't sure if even a building permit would pull him back out.

My heart squeezed in my chest. I closed the fridge door and went over to dig Dad out of the avalanche of clothes. "Hey, Dad! Let's watch something light and fun. Abbot and Costello, maybe. Or Mel Brooks? Buster Keaton?"

"I wanna watch!" Shine shouted. I queued up *The General.* Shine sat on one side of Dad. I elbowed him until he sat up, then slipped into the space beside him. Dad's eyes stared out from his shaggy beard. He looked like Tom Hanks in *Castaway*. He didn't laugh at the funny parts.

The metal steps leading up to the front door rumbled and twanged. A key jingled in the lock. My mother's face creased into a scowl as she looked around the room. "I don't suppose any of you started dinner while I was working my tail off."

Shine and I scrambled off the sofa. "I'd started dinner, but . . ." I began.

My mother stopped me with a lazer-look. "It seems nobody here can finish what they started anymore."

Shine pulled a bag of tortilla chips out of the cabinet. She stuffed one in her mouth.

"You'll ruin your appetite," I whispered.

She shrugged. "Tortilla chips' crunch drowns out the yelling. And there's going to be yelling."

I couldn't argue with that, but I couldn't sit and listen to my mother's shrieking anymore, either. I knew after she finished with Dad, she was going to move on to me. I laced up my P.E. shoes and headed out the door. The theme song from *Chariots of Fire* played in my head. I told myself I was Jesse Owens in *The Jesse Owens Story* and I would overcome all the hardships that began with the fire.

I ran to the sheriff's office. Deputy Chavez was already gone for the day, so I left a message with the receptionist, telling him that I'd been by to check on progress. Then I ran to Tiffany's house, which was all the way across town and up a long hill. Her dad answered the door and told me she was out in the stable.

Tiffany looked up from picking Spunky Jean's hooves. "Oh, hey! I don't get to see you much anymore, now that school's out. I miss you. How's it going?"

"Okay, I guess. How about for you?" The smell of hay and horse and leather hit me hard. I missed it so much it hurt.

"Okay, too. Been busy getting Spunky Jean into shape. Get a new phone yet?"

I shook my head. "My folks keep forgetting. They're bogged down with house rebuilding stuff."

Tiffany raised one eyebrow. "A likely excuse."

I pressed my lips together, not sure if she was accusing my parents of not caring for me, or me of making excuses for my parents. I didn't want to get in a fight with Tiffany. There were too many other people I was mad at. But I couldn't help feeling hurt.

She held out a curry comb. "Want to brush Spunky Jean while I finish her hooves? I can tell you all about how Martina and I did in the last rodeo."

I clasped my hands behind my back. I just couldn't be around another horse right now, especially another bay. Spunky Jean wasn't Wildfire, but they had enough in common that my brain started playing tricks on me. That black tail swishing. The black stockings. My heart pounded in my ears. My feet started to shuffle of their own accord.

Tiffany looked up. "I could use a little help here. Really. It might do you good to be around another horse."

I shook my head and started to back out of the stable.

Tiffany let Spunky Jean's hoof slide off her knee. "Punk? You okay? Forget helping. Let's go in the house. It's almost dinner time. Want to stay?"

"I . . . I gotta get back for dinner," I rushed out the door and ran hard all the way home. I arrived gasping. To find there was no dinner to run home to. Mom had left. Who knew where. Dad was back to staring at the TV. And Shine had eaten the entire bag of tortilla chips and put herself to bed. I crawled into bed myself. I was hot and sticky, and too sick at heart to sleep for a long, long time.

When I woke up, the sky was pink with dawn and my mother was yelling at my dad to get out of bed and feed us girls. I laced up my P.E. shoes again and ran away from the screaming. I didn't know where I was going, and I didn't care. Anywhere was better than the white tin can.

I found myself where our house used to be. It took me almost two hours to get there, and I arrived huffing and puffing, my face streaked with tears I didn't know I had cried. I kicked through the ashes, looking for something, anything that had survived from my old life. Even the ashes had changed. Instead of being powdery and gray like they had been right after the fire, the ashes had mixed themselves into the dirt, swirling, marbled streaks of gray among the red-brown. My toe hit something hard and my heart leaped in my chest. Had I found my rodeo belt buckle? I kicked harder, uncovering not the buckle, but one of Wildfire's old horseshoes. I held it for a long time, staring at it and remembering what it was like when the barn was still here and Wildfire was in it. Rage and frustration built in me until I shook all over. I threw the horseshoe as hard as I could. It spinned through the air like a boomerang. But this boomerang didn't come back. Would anything ever come back around to what it used to be?

I trotted down the road I took on the night of the fire. Then, Wildfire and I moved at a breakneck gallop and the road was packed with cars, all trying to escape but going nowhere. Now, I limped along while the cars tore past me. Tears choked me and I had to stop on the side of the road until I could breathe again.

When I got to town, I checked in at the sheriff's office to see if Ernesto Chavez had any news. The receptionist told me the deputy was out of the office investigating some new case, but he'd add my new message to the pile I'd already left.

I limped over to Jack's Flapjack House, hoping for a place to rest and, maybe, a glass of water. By now the sun was past its zenith and I was so empty and dehydrated that I felt like my belly was touching my spine and my mouth was coated with cardboard.

Sheila, the waitress that served me the day after the fire, smiled at me and pointed towards a booth in the back.

"I don't have any money on me. I was just out for a run," I said.

"Ran out of gas? All us runners have bonked at one time or another. Order what you need. You can pay me later." Sheila poured me a glass of water and left the pitcher on the table so I could refill my glass. The next time she passed, she set a large glass of orange juice on my table and gave me a wink.

I picked up the paper that'd been abandoned in the booth next to me. The fire that destroyed my house wasn't even mentioned. Other fires were raging throughout the drought-ravaged Southwest. Grasslands were blazing in Colorado. There was a picture of a bomber flying over a National Forest on fire in California. Smoke was compromising air quality all along the bosque, the cottonwood forest that lined the Rio Grande. With the entire region ablaze, no one was thinking of Alamitos anymore. We were old news. Forgotten. Ignored.

The run home was hard even though it was all downhill. I tallied up the distances and figured I'd run ten or eleven miles, way longer than my body was used to. I pressed the heel of my hand into my side and pushed on, walking when I had to, running when I could. I hadn't eaten all day. My head ached.

I got home just as the sunset turned the entire western sky a blazing red. I dropped onto the metal stairs, too tired to climb them or turn the doorknob. It had been an especially hot day, so hot that the sweat evaporated on my face. I rubbed a hand across it and felt the salt crystals. Heat radiated into the backs of my legs from the metal stairs. I wondered if they would burn marks into them.

"Punk? That you?" Shine called from the other side of the door.

"It's me," I called back. "Get me a bottle of water, K?"

Shine came out, arching her back so that the two water bottles she clutched to her chest wouldn't fall as she opened the door, stepped through, and fumbled to close it again. It didn't work. I scooped my bottle up on the second bounce as she blew back her bangs and plopped down beside me.

"I hate air conditioning. Keeping all the doors and windows closed. Daddy said it was too hot, even then, so he went to Benny's."

I blinked. Twice. Why hadn't I noticed that Dad's old pickup wasn't parked on the curb? "Dad left you and went to a bar?"

"Uh huh. Open this for me, please."

I took her bottle, gave it a twist until the seal on the cap broke, then handed it back. "How long ago was that?"

"I dunno," Shine said with a shrug. "Lunch time? Only, him and me didn't eat lunch. Not yet." Shine got up and went into the house just as my mother pulled the car up to the curb and opened the car door. Her blouse was rumpled, the fabric stained dark beneath her armpits.

"Air conditioning in the car not working?" I asked.

She blew a stray strand of hair out of her eyes and nodded. "Another thing for your father to ignore. He in there?" She jerked her chin toward the closed door.

I shook my head. "He went to Benny's."

My mother lifted an eyebrow and studied the place where dad's pickup should have been parked. She leaned over and picked up her briefcase. "Your father finally gets off the sofa, and where does he go? To a bar? And leaves you two here alone?"

"Maybe he just wanted to be with people who wouldn't yell at him."

My mother's frown deepened. I shrugged, not wanting to tell her that

Shine had been home alone because I had been gone all day myself. She'd probably self-immolate. One fire ball and poof! Just like the house, nothing left but a pile of ashes, with her high heels sticking up out of them. An image of the Wicked Witch's shoes sticking out from beneath Dorothy's house in the *Wizard of Oz* flashed through my mind.

My mother swayed on her feet. Feeling guilty that I was thinking of my mother as a witch, I leapt up, took the briefcase from her and nudged her gently through the door. Inside, Shine looked up from a can of frosting that she'd been dipping graham crackers into. Her cheeks were smeared with chocolate.

"I'm hungry," she whined.

"How about an apple? Something healthy?" Mother asked.

Shine shrugged. "Aren't any."

My mother looked around the room. The TV droned in the corner. Laundry, clean but unfolded, covered the sofa. The mail lay in an avalanched pile next to the coffee table, the dishes in a similar pile by the sink.

"That's it," my mother said. "Get in the car. We're going to Maureen and Dutch's."

"For dinner?" Shine's voice squeaked with pleasure.

"Yes for dinner. Maybe for the whole weekend. Pack a bag."

My chest tightened. "Shouldn't we wait for Dad to come home?"

"We need a break from Dad," my mother said, then corrected herself. "I need a break from Dad."

"This is only temporary, right? Just a few days apart?" I asked while we buckled in.

"Of course," my mother said. "It's only temporary."

I leaned my head against the glass. If visiting Maureen and Dutch would allow Mother to calm down and stop nagging Dad, it would be worth being away from him, at least for a little while. I looked up, trying to see the first star pop out of the gathering darkness. When I found it, I would make some wishes:

1) That someone would find Wildfire.

2) That Dad would get off the couch and start being a dad again.

3) That life would get back to normal.

But I couldn't see any stars. All I could see was the green reflection of the dashboard.

The car weaved and swayed down the winding mountain road until it came to the flats, where we joined a long line of red tail lights bound for Albuquerque. I brushed back a tear that had slipped from my eye. There were too many loses: first the house, then Wildfire, and now my dad. At least my mother said that this last loss was only temporary. But that's not what she meant at all.

Chapter Seven
Maureen and Dutch
July 15-16

Maureen and Dutch lived in a neighborhood that was thrown up in the big boom that came after World War Two. It'd been going downhill ever since. I pressed my nose to the window to block out the dashboard lights and watched the chain link fences flash past in the headlights. Behind the fences lay dead lawns and dirt patches in front of stucco-covered, flat-roofed houses, all with three-bedrooms and one bath. Some of the nicer ones had one- car garages. Others, including Maureen's, had sagging carports. Even in the darkness, the whole neighborhood looked like it gave up on appearances long ago and was willing to accept its own shabbiness.

Mother pulled up to Maureen's chain-link fence and honked the car horn. The door to Maureen's house flew open and half a dozen mutts and a bunch of cats exploded out in a frenzy of barking, yowling, and tail wagging. Dutch followed close behind. She waded through the dogs, her short gray curls glowing in the headlights like a halo. Dutch opened the gate and my mother drove slowly up the driveway, hoping to avoid running over any of the milling throng. Mother parked next to Maureen's old Mercury Cougar and Dutch's even more ancient looking

Subaru.

"Where's Auntie Maureen? I need a hug," Shine said as she climbed out of the car. I followed, surprised by how stiff and sore my leg muscles were. Then I remembered I'd run probably ten miles that day. It seemed a lifetime ago.

Dutch jerked her chin toward the house. "Your auntie's in the kitchen, Girly Girl. Like always."

My aunt Maureen is much older than my mother. She had been a nurse in Operation Desert Shield, back in the 90s. When my grandparents died in a car wreck, Maureen got an honorable discharge and came back to Albuquerque to raise my mother. There are two boys in between Maureen and my mother, my uncles Howard and Vernon, but both of them moved away as soon as they were old enough. We don't see them very often.

A decade after Maureen came home, Dutch came to live with her until she got on her feet. The years stretched on and Dutch became a permanent fixture. Maureen is a sucker for orphans, divorced friends, lost dogs, and stray cats. Anyone who shows up at her door gets fed. Especially us.

We walked through a front room filled with ancient sofas with floral upholstery, past the dinning room that hadn't been used for anything but the never-ending Monopoly game or jigsaw puzzles for as long as I could remember, and into the kitchen, where the first thing I saw was Maureen's rear end as she bent over to pull a pan out of the oven. I breathed in the warm, comforting smell of cinnamon and felt my shoulders relax. Maureen's kitchen was as tired looking as the rest of the neighborhood. Some of the tiles in the linoleum floor curled, exposing black glue and the underlying plywood. The dining set had aluminum frames, cracked red vinyl seats patched with duct tape, and a white formica tabletop that glinted with gold specks. It looked retro, and had to be older, even, than Maureen. The cabinets had at least fifteen coats of paint on them. I know because Shine and I once spent a rainy day counting the rainbow layers of colors in the nicks and gashes.

Maureen straightened up and turned around, scowling at us over the top of her reading glasses in a way that I knew was totally fake. Her oven-mitt covered hands cradling a bubbling peach cobbler, she stuck out her lower lip and blew a strangling strand of hair out of her eyes.

"Well, look what the cats dragged in. Sit down. You must be half starved."

Maureen jerked her chin toward the kitchen table. Shine and I clambered into chairs and unfolded our napkins. A cat leaped up on the table. Maureen shooed it off with a wave of the serving spoon. The dogs walked around in tight circles, then collapsed with deep, contented sighs.

"Peach cobbler for dinner? You don't have any wine, do you?" My Mother sagged into a seat and accepted the coffee mug Dutch handed her.

"Little late for dinner," Maureen said. "And you know we never have alcohol around. Milk, apple juice, orange juice, coffee: those are your choices."

Dutch nodded. "Let's just get some nice warm comfort food into our girls and pour them into bed. We can worry about nutrition in the morning. Girls, you take the guest room so Lainey can have her old room."

"But I want the room that's pink and lacey!" Shine whined. "The guest bedroom smells like old ladies! And I'll have to share a bed with Punk!"

"You can't always get what you want. Be glad you get a bed at all," Maureen snapped.

Shine stuffed peach cobbler into her mouth instead, burning her tongue. I ate slowly, sipping milk to cool the hot, sticky filling.

Mother set her mug down. Hard. Her nostrils flared. I steeled myself for another rant. "I am so tired of . . ."

Maureen cut her off with a wave of the serving spoon. "We're all tired. Little pitchers . . ."

"Have big ears. Let's get our girls to bed. Then we'll play some Monopoly and talk a bit," Dutch said. Maureen and Dutch had been living together so long that they frequently finished each other's sentences.

I licked the inside of my bowl, getting the last of the thick, sweet filling. When I put it down, Maureen was scowling at me. She pointed the spoon and I thought I was going to get a lecture in table manners, but something different came out. "I'm going to be gone by the time you wake up, so I'll tell you now: steer clear of that boy next door."

"The Montoyas are good people," Dutch added. "Haven't had a lick of trouble from them the whole time they've lived there. But that boy . . ."

"Ain't nothing but trouble." Maureen said. "And I'm getting groceries tomorrow after work. Any dinner requests?"

"Macaroni and cheese!" Shine shouted.

Maureen nodded and looked at me. "Chicken fried steaks still your favorite?"

I nodded, suddenly too tired to even discuss either what I wanted for dinner or the next-door neighbors. Why would I care, anyway? We were only here for a few days. I had never met the Montoyas, so there would be little point in meeting any of them this time.

I yawned and excused myself from the table, waving off Maureen as she tried to ladle a second serving into my bowl. I walked, stiff-legged, back to the guest bedroom, slipped off my shoes and shorts and fell into bed. I'd intended to lie awake and listen to what Dutch, Maureen and my mother talked about. I didn't hear a single word. I never felt my sister slip into bed beside me.

The sound of Maureen's Mercury Cougar woke me. Her car always surprised me. It was a big old muscle car, the kind that showed up in old 1970's shows like *Starsky and Hutch* and *The Dukes of Hazzard*, and its engine growled low and mean like the big cat it was named after. It didn't seem like the kind of car a graying old auntie should drive, especially one who takes in stray cats and makes peach cobbler for her nieces.

I grabbed the alarm clock off the nightstand and squinted at it. Four thirty in the morning. Maureen wasn't kidding when she said she'd be gone when I got up. She and Dutch were both nurses at the VA hospital, and they worked odd hours so that one of them could always be home with the animals. I laid back and stared at the ceiling, waiting for sleep to return, but my leg muscles ached for me to get up and stretch them. After an hour I gave up, threw off the covers and tiptoed out to the front porch, where I nearly stepped on a big black Labrador retriever. The dog looked up, thumped his tail once against the concrete and went back to sleep while I laced up my running shoes. I stretched until my back popped, then headed out.

The stars faded as the sky went from black to gray as I ran down the street. I turned right, then right again, planning to do a ladder through the neighborhood, up one street and down the other. It was cool out here, and birds lazily chirped, greeting the coming dawn. Way off to the east, the Sandia Mountains showed up as a jagged black line. I wondered where Wildfire was, and if he was okay. Maybe when Dutch got up, I could have her help me call to check on the investigation and see whether they had any more clues. I missed brushing him out early in the morning and taking him for a ride as the sky lightened to blue.

When I got back to the house, panting and sweating, the dog looked up again. But he didn't look at me. This time, he looked to the east. He thumped his tail a couple of times and laid his head back down. I took a deep breath, then held it. In the ensuing silence, I heard a dull clang, clang, clang - a bicycle pedal thumping a chain guard with each rotation. A shadowy figure rolled into the Montoya's yard. I watched it pull up to the garage and touch a key pad, then the garage door hummed up. For a moment, the garage light illuminated his face. He was young: about my age, with long, stringy hair held back with a wide bandana, kind of like Ralph Macchio in *The Karate Kid,* one of the movies that me and dad liked to watch together. He reached back, hitched up his sagging khakis, then disappeared into the dim cavern.

I snorted. What could be so bad about a boy who got up early to go for a bike ride? If only he were riding a horse instead of a bike, he'd be perfect. I peered back over my shoulder to make sure Dutch wasn't up yet. The house was dark, so I slipped off the porch and through the gate to see more about this bad boy I'd been warned about.

By the time I stood at the open garage door, the boy had his handle bars off and was taking off the bike's seat.

"Hi," I said.

The boy fell back. His wrench twirled through the air, clattered against a bicycle frame that hung from the rafters, then dropped down, hitting him on the head. I let out a little scream, then clamped my hand over my mouth. We froze for a moment, both of us wide-eyed with shock, panting, staring at each other. He put a hand on his head and winced, then pulled up the bandana that had settled over his eyes.

"*Madre de dios*," he muttered, picking himself off the ground. "Don' never scare me like that."

"Sorry," I piped, my voice no more than a squeak.

He shook his wrench at me. "Lucky I didn' have no gun on me. You would'a been dead, Chica."

"I only wanted to say hi."

"Well, you done that. *Mierda.*" The boy reached back and pulled up his sagging khakis again, then squatted down and returned to unscrewing the bike seat. Now that I could see him, he really was kind of cute. His hair was almost black, but his eyes were a clear, light greenish gray.

"I'm Margaret, but everyone calls me Punk."

He studied me for a moment, then went back to working on his bike. "Nobody calls me punk and gets away with it."

"It's short for Pumpkin. Because of my hair," I stammered. Shut up, I told myself. I must sound like an idiot.

He looked up again, and smiled. "Pumpkin, huh? *¿Que te pasa, calabaza?*"

"Huh?" I stared.

He let out a little snort. "Spanish. It means, what's up, pumpkin?"

"Oh. I get it. I'm visiting my aunt. She lives next door." I jerked my head, indicating which house

"Yeah? Which is your tia, Chica? The big girly one or the little butch?"

I blinked, startled by this question. "Maureen and Dutch aren't lesbians."

He shrugged. "Don't matter to me if they are or not. People can do whatever they want."

I turned on my heel and marched out of there. Maureen and Dutch were right; this boy was nothing but bad news and I didn't want to have anything more to do with him. The more I thought about it, the more agitated I felt. All these years, and I had never questioned the relationship between Maureen and Dutch. They were just simply Maureen and Dutch. I already had enough to deal with. Why did this kid have to go and bring up one more thing for my mind to wrestle with?

I slammed the kitchen door as I came through it. Dutch looked up from the bowl she had tucked under her arm. The kitchen smelled of bacon and maple syrup and the pile of fresh squeezed orange halves that sat on the drain board.

"Had fun talking with our little reprobate?" she asked.

I dropped into a chair. "You were right. He is a jerk."

Dutch nodded. "You could have just trusted us on that and saved yourself the grief. Some people have to learn the hard way."

I slumped back in my chair and watched Dutch mix the pancake batter. She was short and square, with short cropped gray hair that stood out from her head like an SOS pad, and round, wire-framed glasses the same color as her hair. Over her powder blue scrubs, she wore the frilly apron which I knew was Maureen's.

"Hey, Dutch? It's with a D, right? Like the little Dutch girl? Why do we call you that?"

Dutch looked up. "That juvenile delinquent call me something different?"

I shook my head no, mumbling some lame excuse that I could tell she didn't believe. Dutch began beating the tar out of the batter making the skin on the back of her arm flap. These were going to be tough pancakes.

"No one calls me it anymore, but the name on my driver's license is Janneke Aelberdijnck. It's a good Dutch name. My people came over from Holland in the 60s. When I was in the Army, that was the name that was right here, on my name tape, on my uniform." Dutch drew two fingers across her left breast. "Girly girl, if you were a GI's just been brought in on a stretcher, all shot to hell and back, you want to call me Nurse Aelberdijnck? Or Dutch?"

"Got it," I said, chuckling.

She poured the batter onto the griddle in a long, sizzling stream. "Your aunt and I went to hell and back, too, during the war. She lost her fiancé, and I came home with a husband who couldn't forget what he'd been through. Kept living it over and over. Finally got so violent I had to escape before he hurt me."

I nodded, dumbfounded by ideas I'd never thought of before. "Maureen had a fiancé?"

With a flourish, Dutch flipped the pancakes high in the air. One missed the skillet and hit the ground, where it disappeared behind a scurry of dogs. "Nice young man, too. Helicopter pilot. Met him over there. She and Bob, Bruce and I used to double date when we were all in camp together. Then your grandparents died and Maureen came back to take care of Lainey, who was still in grade school. There's fourteen years between them, you know. From then on, most people just thought Maureen was Lainey's mom.

"Maureen hadn't been gone more than two months when Bob got ambushed trying to medevac wounded. He made it back to base, but just barely. We shipped him back in a body bag a week later. Got a medal of honor for it, if that's any consolation. Bruce rotated out a year after that, and me six months after him. Then we got married. Didn't last very long. After all that, is it any wonder that me and Maureen cling to each other for comfort?"

Dutch set the platter of pancakes in front of me. Her gray blue eyes flashed challenges through the lenses of her glasses. I shook my head no. After all that, Dutch and Maureen had every right to piece together any sort of life they could, no questions asked.

"Look at this place," Dutch said, wiping her hands on the apron. "Ain't much to look at, but it's full of love. Maybe that punk next door should come and have a look-see before he starts judging things that aren't any of his business. Now, I'm going to 'rise my Shine' and you get your mama up. After breakfast, she's going in to fix a few things with the lab and I'm taking my girls to the library. Got a friend there I want you to meet."

Chapter Eight
Sympathy and Guys
July 16

My mother showed up at the breakfast table in her brown suit and pumps.

"Got a meeting with the big brass?" I asked.

"Is it that obvious? Dutch, you got any yogurt? My stomach's too nervous for all that sugar. Yes, Punkin, fingers crossed I can expedite some changes that will make life run more smoothly."

"Whose life run more smoothly?" I asked.

My mother didn't respond. She jerked open the refrigerator door, studied the contents, then shut it again. "Forget it. I'm just taking this banana and a cup of coffee."

"Want a sack lunch?" Dutch asked, but my mother was already out the door and trying to make it to the car without getting slobbered on by one of the dogs. I walked out with her so I could open and close the gate.

"She going to push the lab into expediting our building permit?" I asked when I reentered the kitchen and took my place next to Shine, who was shoveling in pancakes while reading the back of a cereal box.

"And you think the lab can do that how?" Dutch poured me a big glass of orange juice and set it on the kitchen table.

I shrugged. "I don't know how any of these agencies work. But if she gets that permit, then she won't have to worry about what Dad is doing – or not doing – anymore, and she can focus on her lab work and her reports. That's what they want, right?"

"You've got a point," Dutch said.

"If she gets that permit, we won't be here very long," I said. "Not long enough for a trip to the library." We only went to the library near Maureen and Dutch's house when we were staying a week or more, like over Christmas break or during summer vacation. A trip to the library meant that Dutch didn't think Mother's brown suit and most businesslike attitude would move things along as fast as I wanted.

"However long you're staying, you need something to keep you busy," Dutch said.

"I'll brush my teeth! Then I'll be ready!" Shine pushed the cereal box away. As soon as she'd left the room, Dutch sat in Shine's seat and finished eating the syrupy bits and pieces of bacon and pancakes that were left on Shine's plate. I don't think I've ever seen Dutch start with her own, clean plate, except maybe at Thanksgiving.

"Girly, girl, you may be here a while. Your mother and father have more to work out than just building permits," Dutch said in a low voice between bites.

I frowned. My mother and dad hadn't made much of a commitment to finding Wildfire. They'd been too overwhelmed with all the other things they had to deal with. But if I was ever going to find him, I needed to search now. The longer I waited, the farther they might have taken him, the colder any leads. Dad needed us, too. I pictured him sitting up there in that white metal box they called temporary housing. Without us, he had no reason to turn off the tv and get off the sofa. Dad needed us to push him back into lines for our building permits and our construction materials. That was the first step in rebuilding not only a house, but our family. Staying with Maureen and Dutch would not accomplish that.

We climbed into Dutch's Subaru and immediately Shine started bouncing up and down on the vinyl seat. Shine loved libraries. She loved the reaction she got from librarians when she checked out an immensely tall stack of books. She loved returning them, proudly mentioning details from each just so they would know she'd actually read them all. I'm not the reader Shine is. Like my dad, I'd rather watch a movie than read a book. I jiggled my knee back and forth and picked at my cuticles.

"There it is!" Shine shouted, pointing to the sculpture that stood in the median on the street outside the library. It was a big pile of letters, all made out of metal and looking like they'd tumble any minute, but that pile had looked just like that for as long as I could remember. Not everything changes.

We pulled into the library's parking lot. Dutch pointed to the public pool next door. It was already full of shrieking kids and coaches with whistles. "Remember taking swim lessons there last summer, Shine? Shall we see if they have some openings for next week or the week after?"

"Cool beans!" Shine squealed with delight. "And can we pack a lunch and play at the park?"

Dutch nodded. "Maybe this fall you can play on one of the soccer teams that practices here."

"No, she can't. We won't be here that long. This is only temporary." I got out, slammed the door, and headed to the library before Dutch could argue. I jerked the library door open and stormed in. It was dark and cool inside, and I stood there, blinking like an owl in the daylight as I tried to calm down.

The woman who sat at the circulation desk looked up over the top of a pair of bright turquoise reading glasses, her mouth pursed into a little round O. One of her perfect eyebrows arched as if asking me what I was doing here. Looking at how her curly hair was piled elaborately atop her head, and how her garnet fingernails matched her garnet blouse, I wondered that myself. I coughed and awkwardly pulled some of the wrinkles out of my shirt. The door opened behind me, and Dutch and Shine entered. The woman's gaze went from me, to Dutch and then back to me and her mouth split into a toothy smile that was almost goofy, melting her professional iciness.

"Hola, Dutch," the woman said, "these your nieces?"

"Yup. My girls. This is Sadie, but we call her Shine, and this is Margaret. We call her Punkin. Girls, say hi to Mercedes Escudero. She's the most knowledgeable librarian in the whole state."

"Wanna help me pick out some books?" Shine asked, bouncing up to the desk. She smiled, her face flushed with the joy of meeting someone she assumed loved books as much as she did. It made my stomach sour.

How could Shine be so happy when we were so far away from Dad?

Dutch put a hand on Shine's shoulder. "I know where to find your books. Let's let Mercedes help Punk, okay?"

The two of them moved off towards the kiddie section, leaving me to glare at Mercedes on my own. I'd seen her smile before, on dozens of relief workers and government officials. It meant that Dutch had talked to her about us already. She probably knew our whole, sad story. I hated being set up like this. After a few minutes she cleared her throat and began talking in a voice that was too enthusiastic.

"Punkin? Isn't it time you outgrow that nickname? Us women have a hard enough time getting people to take us seriously. I hear you like horses. Ever read *Black Beauty*?"

"No, but I saw the movie. Unlike my life, it's about a girl who saves her horse from a fire and everything actually turns out okay."

Mercedes winced. "Well, not exactly."

"Whatever," I said. "I'm not much of a reader, anyway. Me and my Dad, we're old movie fans."

"We've got a great DVD selection." She pointed over her shoulder.

"I'm not really interested in watching movies right now. Not without my dad."

Mercedes nodded as if she understood, which she couldn't. "So, what can I help you with?"

I sighed. "Getting out of here. Finding my horse. Getting back to normal." The more I said, the harder the lump that formed in the middle of my chest. I bit my lip, afraid that if I didn't shut up, I would start to cry, and the realization that I might cry in front of this totally professional stranger made me hate her even more.

Mercedes scooted back her chair. "Sounds like internet research would be better for you than fiction. Let's see what we can find. Can I sign you up for a computer access card?"

I shook my head. "I'm not going to be in town more than a day or two."

Mercedes nodded. "Let's not bother, then. Let's use mine." Before I knew it, she was around the desk and at my side. She took my elbow and gently guided me toward a quiet nook that was filled with carrels. A computer screen glowed out of each carrel. Mercedes pulled up two chairs to one monitor. She motioned for me to sit down, then pulled the keyboard close and logged on.

"Hey! *¿Que te pasa, calabaza?*" I stiffened. That jerk Montoya boy. I turned to scowl at him, hoping he'd get the message and leave.

"Hey! My man, Paco. How're ya doing?" Mercedes held out her fist and she and Paco bumped knuckles.

"Same ol, same ol," Paco said, hauling up his khakis. He talked to Mercedes, but looked directly at me and smiled. Jerk.

"Well, get to it." Mercedes pointed one of those perfectly manicured fingernails at a computer on the other side of the nook. Paco nodded, then strolled to it.

"You know him?" I whispered.

"Paco doesn't have a computer at the Montoya's. He comes here to work on an online class," Mercedes whispered back.

I gasped. "A class? During the summer?"

Mercedes nodded. "His schooling's been a bit disrupted, so he's got some make-up to do. But he'll catch up. He's a smart kid. Now, what do we want to search for?"

I snorted. His too-big pants sagging down and his too-wide bandana getting in the way of his eyes made him look just plain stupid: a caricature of a tough young dude, kind of like the kids in *The Outsiders.* Even if those eyes were the most amazing color.

"I want to search for my horse," I said. "Wildfire was stolen by some lady who said she was from the Equine Assistance League and nobody seems to be able to find them or him. How do we start looking?"

Mercedes googled "Equine Assistance League." A number of animal welfare groups came up, but there were no complete matches. We found a Trudy Goodheart, a small business owner in Texas. but her Facebook picture looked nothing like the woman who'd met me in the parking lot. Typing in "Recovering stolen horses" brought up an organization called *Stolen Horse International*, which explained that since it was difficult to track a stolen horse once it had been through a sale yard, the people who stole horses tried to sell them quickly. Since thieves didn't care about what happened to the horse, many horses ended up going to slaughter.

My shoulders sagged. "Not Wildfire. They can't do that to him."

"Not to worry. Your auntie tells me he was young and healthy. It's likely he'd be resold as a riding mount for some stable."

"She's not my auntie," I said, crossing my arms across my chest.

"She's my aunt's friend." I was so angry that I wanted to say girlfriend, not friend, but I just couldn't cross that divide yet. Not even with people who bring me to the library and dump me with over-enthusiastic power-women like Mercedes.

Mercedes pointed at the screen. "Look here. It says they also help owners who lost their horses during natural disasters such as wildfires and hurricanes. If they reunited pet owners with pets after Hurricane Leonora, they can help you. And here they mention a book you might want to read. I'm going to put it on the request list so the library will buy it, but I'll get a copy through inter-library loan to tide us over until then. I've got some other work to do, too. Look through the site. Get some ideas about what you want to do next. I'll check back with you in a while."

Mercedes pushed back her chair. "I own a couple of horses. I can't imagine how upset I'd be if someone stole Navajo or Galadriel. They're my babies," she said in a voice that dripped with sympathy.

The title of the book was *Horse Theft. Been There—Done That.* I scrolled through the table of contents, looking for clues as to what to do. I stopped scrolling, my hand frozen on the mouse. Chapter 2 had a subheading entitled *Equine Slaughter Facilities.* I groaned and buried my face in my hands. The thought that this Goodheart woman might have sold Wildfire to a slaughter house where he'd be turned into dog food was too much. All the frustrations and fears that I'd been holding down ever since the fire bubbled up in a flood of tears. I could no more hold them back than I could have held back those flames when they came over the ridge that night.

"Hey, Chica, don' cry." Paco slipped into the chair next to me. His voice was gentle, comforting. I leaned my head against the table, surrendering my pride to despair.

"I can't help it," I sobbed through my fingers.

"You wan' we should get out of here, Chica? Get some air?"

Five minutes before, I would have told him no. Five minutes before I'd thought of Paco as a jerk who I wanted nothing to do with. But all that had changed. The words *Equine Slaughter Facilities* had made me feel so alone, so helpless that I welcomed company, even his.

"They aren't lesbians," I said weakly.

He nodded. "I'm sorry I teased you. Let me make it up to you now."

Paco put his hand on the small of my back and guided me. He pulled a couple of tissues from the box on the inquiry desk as we passed. We were out the door and I was blowing my nose on those tissues before Mercedes or Dutch or anyone else noticed that we were gone.

As he worked on unlocking his bike, Paco shushed me with little Spanish mutterings. Perhaps they were the kind of things one said to a hysterical child, perhaps he was doing nothing but cursing. I didn't know. What I did know was that his tone was neither uncaring or overly, drippily sympathetic like all those relief workers. Once he had the bike free, he gestured towards the handlebars.

"Get on, Chica."

I stared at him. "Where're we going?"

"No worries. You'll be back before your Tia even knows you're gone."

His bike was one of those strange, patch-together jobs. It had little wheels and a big, banana seat, and handlebars that curved up like the kind on Dennis Hopper's motorcycle in *Easy Rider.*

"I'm too heavy," I said, but he glared at me in a way that broached no argument. I settled my butt into the bottom of the handlebars and wrapped my arms around the handles as if they were the chains on a swing. Paco stepped down on the pedal. The bike wobbled. I panicked, my legs jerking out straight in front of me, but then I settled in and placed my feet on top of each other on the front fender. We headed uphill on the path into the park. Paco's breathing became ragged. He stood on the pedals and pushed them down hard. We clattered over a wooden-slatted bridge that spanned the arroyo. At the top of the park he turned, then turned again, right into the concrete-lined arroyo. It was a straight shot downhill, and Paco pushed himself to gain speed. The wind spread my tears across my temples and cooled my face. Paco turned the bike so we climbed halfway up one embankment, then turned the handlebars and we raced across and up the other side. We zigzagged back and forth, speeding up on the downhills, slowing on the ups. Laughter bubbled out of me the same way tears had – quickly and without my willing it. We popped up the side of the arroyo and wheeled across the library's parking lot, right up to the entrance.

"Later," Paco said as I got off. As I watched him go back the way we had come, I put a hand to my face. The tears were gone, but salt crystals remained. I rubbed them off, then went back into the library. Mercedes looked up from the desk as I entered.

"You okay?"

"Yeah," I said. "Just taking a little break."

"That's good," she said. She didn't know just how good it was.

Chapter Nine
Biding Time
July 17

Sometime in the middle of the afternoon Maureen and Dutch had what we all called 'the changing of the guard.' Maureen came home and Dutch left for work. I opened and closed the gate for each of them, saluting as smartly as a soldier as they passed by, then settled in to pass the time until we could go back to Alamitos and Dad. While Shine watched Tom chase Jerry on TV, I spent the lazy late afternoon brushing burrs out of dog coats, clipping cat claws and cleaning litter boxes. Although it wasn't the same as currying Wildfire's mane, teasing out pads of matted hair made me feel good. I talked with each animal as I worked. Some of them looked at me as if they could actually understand me. Others cringed as I talked, or even growled at me. I wondered if they had been abused. Some of them, I knew, had been. Their badly cropped ears proved it. Or their scars. If animals could talk, I'm sure we'd all learn a lot more about human cruelty than we'd really like to learn.

I brushed a little, ginger-colored mutt who was probably part golden retriever. My thoughts wandered to Wildfire. I hoped that no one was mistreating him. Mercedes had said that he was too valuable to be sold for slaughter, and that he'd most likely been sold to a riding stable. I thought about what that stable might look like, what kind of people would go to it. Maybe somewhere he was getting brushed right now, like I was brushing these dogs. I hoped that somewhere a girl was talking to him in a soothing, gentle voice as she ran her fingers through his black mane, carefully teasing out the tangles. How long before Wildfire forgot me? How long before the memory of my voice faded? Before he thought that this new girl was the only one who had ever loved him? I hoped it would take a long, long time. Wildfire was smart. He would wonder where I'd gone, how come I'd sold him. But then I felt selfish for wanting him to be as miserable without me as I was without him. I shook my head, trying to dislodge the bad thoughts. Then I focused on the animals in front of me.

Outside, a cicada droned in the mulberry tree. Clouds built into bulbous towers in a sky so blue it hurt to look at. I crossed my fingers and hoped that it would rain. If the monsoons finally came, maybe the forests would stop burning. Maybe then life would get back to normal.

As if there was any such thing as normal any more.

My mother's Volvo pulled up just about dinner time. She honked her horn and Shine ran out to open the gate. They came back in together, surrounded by a swirling crowd of yowling cats and yipping dogs.

"Looks like your ark needs feeding, sis," My mother grabbed a diet cola from the fridge, slipped into a chair and kicked off her pumps.

"Punk, you want to handle that for me? Punk's been playing vet all afternoon," Maureen said.

"More like animal groomer," I said. All I'd done was routine maintenance, smoothing rough coats and hurt feelings. Out on the porch, I pried the cover off the five-gallon paint bucket that held the dry dog food. I ladled a cup into each of a half dozen tin plates and set them on the floor, then headed into the laundry room, where I filled small tin cups with cat food and lined them up atop the washer. When all the animals were fed, I returned to the kitchen, where Shine was bouncing up and down.

"We've been having such fun!" Shine said. "We went to the library, and Dutch let me get six books! An' tomorrow she's taking me to the zoo. And Maureen promised to take me to the Balloon Museum the day after!"

This was a regular vacation for Shine.

"Great. Now set out silverware and plates, will ya?" I said as I poured glasses of milk.

Maureen placed a platter of fried chicken and a basket of biscuits on the table, then rooted around in the fridge, bringing out a bowl of coleslaw. We all took our seats. "Well, well, Lainey. You look like the cat who swallowed the canary," Maureen said.

My mother's mouth turned up in the corners in a tight, satisfied smile, the kind that didn't show any teeth.

"Got some things worked out with the big brass?" I asked, passing some of Maureen's creamy coleslaw.

"Yup." The smile on my mother's face was encouraging. My mother worked on some pretty important projects. Maybe she had convinced someone that our house plans needed to be approved quickly so that she could focus on her work.

I smiled at Shine and passed her the biscuits. "Hope you don't feel too bad if you don't get all those trips to the zoo and museum in."

"Oh, she'll get them," my mother said. "I'm sure Maureen and Dutch will still take her. And there's always weekends."

"We're not going to drive down here every weekend." My stomach clenched in a tight fist. Something was wrong here.

"Won't have to," my mother said. "Larry's packing up my office. I'll be ready to roll by next week."

"Ready to roll what?" I asked. This made no sense. I'd heard Larry's name before. He worked in the same complex as my mother. They often worked on projects together. But why would he pack up her office?

My mother put down her drumstick. She looked at me as if I were a moron. "Punkin, I'll be ready to resume work. I talked with the director of operations today. He agreed to let me continue my research down here. They're setting up a new office for me now. Larry's packing up the papers in my desk and file cabinets and will drive it down tomorrow. By Monday, I'll be able to pick up where I left off."

"We're going to live with Maureen and Dutch forever?" Shine asked.

My mother took a deep breath and let it out in a long, drawn-out sigh. "No, sweetheart. This weekend I'll start looking for a place of our own. A three-bedroom apartment with a pool. Even though he's staying in Alamitos, Larry and I will continue working together. Through video conferencing."

"We're getting a pool?" Shine squeaked.

"But what about Dad?" I asked, my voice right on the edge of hysteria.

"And Schrodinger? Can he come live with us?" Shine asked.

I shot dagger eyes at Shine. Didn't she understand that Schrodinger counted for next to nothing, especially compared with Dad and Wildfire?

"You can't even get me a new phone," I snapped. "What makes you think you should get a new place to live?'

"I can't go back to that hot box!" My mother's voice rose until it was almost a shriek.

Maureen glared at me as if I'd caused my mother's nerves to snap. "What do you need a phone for? You don't even drive. We didn't get Lainey a phone until she was in high school."

"Times change! And I'm not Lainey," I shouted so loud that everyone froze. My shoulders twitched. Blood pounded in my ears.

Maureen sighed and put her hand over mine. "Calm down, Punk. The last few months have put a lot of stress on everybody. I'm sure this weekend, your mom will be able to get a replacement for your phone." Maureen pitched her voice to be low and soothing. Nothing she could say would sooth me right now. I'd lost my house and my horse and my dad, and the stupid phone, and no one seemed to care. My face felt as if it were on fire.

"And just how am I supposed to look for Wildfire from down here?" I asked.

"Dutch said Mercedes was helping you with that," Maureen said.

I glared at her. "Mercedes is just another high and mighty professional who thinks too highly of herself, like the people at the Sheriff's office and the social workers up in Alamitos. She won't really help, unless it makes her look good." I took in a big, shaky breath, afraid that I was going to burst into tears. This was not the short little visit that I thought it was going to be. The visit – and my problems – weren't going to be over any time soon.

Chapter Ten
Joining the Posse
July 18

Back at home, when I had Wildfire to take care of, it was worth getting up early. Here? What's the point? Still, my eyes popped open when the whole city still slumbered in the shadow of the Sandia Mountains and the sky was pearly gray.

I pulled on a pair of shorts and tiptoed out of my room. One of the stray dogs in the kitchen looked up and thumped his tail against the linoleum. Maureen and Dutch must have trained the dogs and cats not to wake the household up whenever anyone stirs. With their weird schedules, it's kind of imperative.

I crept out onto the front porch. Just like in Alamitos, the air was chilly. Dad once told me the air's so thin and dry, it can't hold heat. He said that nights stay hot all summer long down at sea level, and I should be glad to live in a place that can have 40-degree temperature swings. Glad or not, I wished I had brought a sweatshirt with me. I tied on my running shoes, jumped the fence so I didn't have to fight with the gate, and took off down the street to do the same ladder I'd done yesterday. If I closed my eyes, the cool air and the silence were enough to make me think I was back in Alamitos.

When I returned, light was spilling out the bottom of the Montoya's garage door. I walked over and leaned my ear against the cool metal. *Click, click, click*, then a steady *whirrrrr*. Someone inside was working on bike gears. I didn't want to wake anyone in the house, so I knocked really softly.

Bwaaaaang.

It's stupid to even try to knock softly on a metal garage door. It sounds like that giant hitting the gong at the beginning of all old Pinewood Studios movies.

The *click, whirrrrr* inside the garage stopped abruptly. I waited, my heart pounding in my ears, trying to decide whether I should run away or admit what an idiot I was.

"Que tal?" a voice asked. It was Paco, whispering on the other side of the door.

"Paco? It's me," I whispered back.

It was quiet for a moment, and then he pulled the door up. "*Mierda*, Chica. You scared the *caca* out of me. I thought you were the cops or somet'in'."

"The cops?" I asked.

He shrugged and pulled me in, then lowered the door. "Don' matter none. What you doin' up so early?"

"Couldn't sleep."

Paco went back to the bike he was working on. It was a ten speed that he had upside down, resting on its handlebars and seat. He gave the wheel a spin and it made the *whrrrr* I'd heard before. "Somet'in' on your mind?"

I sat down on the little concrete step into the house and let my story go. It was a long, rambling tale. Aside from a few times when he nodded or grunted an acknowledgement, Paco listened silently as he tinkered with the gears.

I threw up my hands. "I don't think I can stand this anymore. Maybe I should just run away."

Paco stopped tinkering and frowned at me. "You ever done that before?"

"No," I answered. "But how hard can it be? You throw a few things in a backpack, and off you go."

"Where you gonna go, Chica?" he asked.

I shrugged. "Anywhere would be better than here."

"How you gonna get food?"

"Buy it?" I asked.

"With what money? For how long?"

I sighed in exasperation. "What makes you an expert?"

"Never mind." His eyes went back to the rotating wheel.

We sat in silence for so long that my butt went numb on the concrete step. Paco kept working on the gears until he got them just the way he wanted them. He gave a satisfied sigh, flipped the bike over, and rolled it over to lean up against the wall. I got up and dusted my butt, trying to wake it up again. I was almost ready to go back over to Maureen and Dutch's when the door to Paco's house opened and a lady that I guessed was Paco's mother stuck her head into the garage.

"Eeeee," she said, looking at me. "Paco, I didn't know you kept girls out here."

"Jus' one," Paco said with a grin.

"You ready for something to eat?"

"Yeah. I'm starved."

"You too?" the lady asked, looking at me.

"Hi, Mrs. Montoya. I'm Margaret Davis. I'm visiting next door." I held out my hand. Paco's mother didn't shake it. She studied me, her eyes narrowed as she thought. Finally, she brightened.

"Oh, I get it. You're Lainey's kid," she said. "And don't call me Mrs. Montoya. I'm Lluvia." She jerked her head toward the kitchen behind her. "Come in and get somet'in' to eat."

We ate *huevos*, which are eggs, and *papas*, which are potatoes, and *tortillas*, which are tortillas. We talked about the neighborhood and how it's gone to seed, and how hard it is to find a good job if you don't finish school (a topic that I'm guessing Lluvia was extra-enthusiastic on for Paco's sake,) and how nice Maureen and Dutch were as neighbors.

I was mopping up the last of the egg yolk with my tortilla when Lluvia threw back her head and cackled with laughter. "Now, don' go telling Dutch how much I fed you. Dutch likes to cook for people. She finds out you got no room in your belly because I fed you first, she'll be mad at me, no?"

I shook my head. "I promise you: whatever Dutch serves up for breakfast, I'll eat. And I won't tell her that your huevos were better."

Dutch looked up as soon as I walked in the door. "Have a good walk? Hope you're hungry. I made you biscuits and gravy."

"My favorite." I slipped into my chair, determined to act famished.

"You going to the zoo with Shine and me?" she asked.

I shook my head. I hadn't finished my plate yet, and I was already so stuffed that all I wanted to do was lay around and groan. I crashed on the sofa when they left. I was still laying around when the droning started.

It began as a low roar: so low that I almost thought I imagined it.

Then it built.

I wasn't imagining it.

It was real.

The sound that I had grown used to in Alamitos had followed me here, to Dutch and Maureen's and it was growing louder by the second.

My legs twitched. My feet tapped a frenetic rhythm against the arm of the sofa. The tanker plane crossed between me and the sun, throwing me momentarily into its loud, rumbling shadow. It flew right over the house, low and slow, the deep rumbling of its propellers reverberating in my chest. The dogs started howling. I leaped off the sofa and out the door.

I ran east. Towards the mountains. Away from the sound.

As I ran, my mind shouted at me. It was time to do something, to make some decisions on my own. Ever since the fire, I'd been waiting for adults to fix everything, waiting for them to make all the right decisions that would get my life back on track. Nothing had gotten fixed, and what few decisions had been made had been wrong ones. I still had no house. No phone. No Wildfire. Dad was still mentally and emotionally AWOL, and now my mother had decided to move to Albuquerque permanently. That meant a new school, a new apartment, a new life. But it fixed nothing. A new life wasn't going to replace all I had lost in the old one. I didn't want a new life. I wanted my old one back, and if the adults in my life weren't going to do anything about it, then I would have to.

By the time I got to a big street, the drone that had followed me from Alamitos, that filled my head with useless fuzz, had faded behind me. The hum of car engines took its place. It was time to get moving. But where? And how?

The street was the kind with businesses, not houses on it, with two lanes going each way and a median filled with dirt and glittering glass shards. I stopped to catch my breath, wait for the light to change, and decide what to do next. Cars zipped by, each one bathing me in a wave of hot, smelly exhaust. Down the street, the jumble of metal letters, the statue that stood in front of the library, glinted in the reflections of the sun cast by passing windshields.

I ran toward it. My stomach felt heavy and queasy from the jumble of biscuits and huevos and gravy and papas. The library had a bathroom. Decision one: use it.

The library also had air conditioning. The frigid air hit my sweaty skin with an arctic blast. Goosebumps broke out on my arms and legs. Mercedes looked up from behind the help desk. The morning sun shone off her glasses, making her eyes unreadable, but her mouth curled up in that goofy smile of hers. She waved that perfectly manicured hand at me. "Good morning, Margaret. How are we today?"

"I don't know how you are, but I need the bathroom," I answered. Mercedes nodded and pointed in a direction I already knew. After I'd done what I went in to accomplish, I splashed water on my face, rinsing off the salt and bringing down the color. When I walked out, Mercedes looked up again. "There now," I said, "we're feeling better. And we've made a decision."

Mercedes furrowed her brow and tried to look serious, but I could see my snarky attitude amused her. "And what decision have we made?"

"We've decided that we need a computer access card, so we can get on the internet, even when it's your day off. And we want to get back on the *Stolen Horse International* website and file a report. I might need your help to do that."

Mercedes nodded and handed me a sheet of paper. "I can do that. I've got to get these books checked in first, though. Here's the internet application. Use your auntie's address on it. And our buddy Paco's here, if you want to say hi."

I took the form and wandered back to the computer area. Paco sat facing the door, but he was so focused on the screen that he didn't notice me as I slipped around the edge of the room and got behind him. Rows of cards glowed on the screen. Paco's mouse clicked as he moved cards into stacks. "*Que pasa*? It's me, the *calabaza*," I said, touching his shoulder.

Paco twitched and pulled the earbuds out of his ears. Spider solitaire disappeared, replaced by a woman who was frozen, her mouth open in what probably was the middle of a lecture. Algebra equations were on the whiteboard beside her.

"Chica! I didn't hear you coming! I was concentrating on my droning teacher." He pointed at the screen.

"Liar. You were playing spider solitaire." I pulled up a chair and sat down.

Paco shrugged again. "Algebra is boring."

"And spider solitaire isn't?"

Paco sighed and leaned back, his fingers laced together over his flat belly. "It's always the same: I start to do my algebra, but all this stuff keeps swirling around in my head, and I need to clear it out so I can concentrate. So, I play a little solitaire. Just one round, I tell myself. But if I win, then it feels good and I play some more. If I lose, I feel bad. I don't want to be a loser, so I play again. I tell myself I'll quit when I'm ahead. And before I know it, three hours have passed and it's time for me to go home."

"Sounds like you're addicted," I said.

"Maybe I am, Chica. My mind keeps telling me, maybe if I get all the cards played just right, maybe everything else in my life will fall into place."

I chuckled and shook my head. "Solitaire isn't life."

"No," he admitted. "But it's hope. And having hope, even if it's in the wrong thing, feels better than having no hope at all."

I waved my hand through the air, batting away his crazy ideas. "Hope isn't going to get you caught up in school. Working on your algebra: that will do it. You've got to stop kidding yourself. You've got to focus."

Paco rolled his eyes. "You sound like Lluvia."

I grinned back. "Then maybe you should listen to the both of us. - Now, you get working on your algebra. I'm going to fill out this application for internet access, and then I'm going to post a missing horse report on *Stolen Horse International.* I bet I finish before you do."

Paco's face lit up. "A bet! Last one done has to push the pedals on the way home, and winner rides on the handlebars!" He stuck his earbuds in his ears, turned back to the screen, and the lady on the screen's mouth started flapping. I smiled. Maybe I could solve Paco's problems as well as my own.

Mercedes registered me so that I could use the library's computers, then she helped some lady with a bunch of whiny kids while I went to

Stolen Horse International. Instead of bogging down on the sad testimonials of lost horses that were turned into dog food, I clicked on the green button that allowed me to post a lost horse, and found myself on another webpage called *Netposse: Missing, Lost, Stolen Pet Database.* I scrolled through a menu that listed different tabs for dogs, horses, and even rabbits. I was filling out the form when I sensed someone behind me, looking over my shoulder. I glanced back and found Mercedes right there, leaning forward so that her big, dangly earrings brushed my cheek. She smelled tropical, like a mix of fruit and flowers. It was a nice smell, and not at all as professional as I'd expect from her.

"I see you've made progress," she said. "Do you have a picture of Wildfire on your phone that you could download? That would help people identify him."

"I don't have a phone," I said. "Not anymore. Lost it in the fire."

"Maybe Lainey has a picture? Or your dad?"

"I can ask. And remind them both that I still need a replacement. I mean, I think insurance paid for it, but my parents just haven't gotten around to replacing it. They've had an awful lot of things to do." I clamped my lips together, angry at myself for making excuses for them. They could have gotten me a new phone if they'd really wanted to.

"If Dutch has one in a frame or something, we could scan it," Mercedes said. She tapped her fingernail on the computer screen, right where it said *Gender: Gelding/Breed: Bay.* "You know, my Galadriel is a bay, too, but a mare. Navajo's a little paint pony. You should come visit. If you can't find any pictures of Wildfire, maybe we could substitute one of Galadriel. That is, if you think they look enough alike."

I clamped my lips together even tighter. I still didn't want to be around other people's horses, especially bays. I'd already been through this with Tiffany.

Paco appeared at my other shoulder. "Done, Chica! And hungry! It's dinner time. Guess who gets to push the pedals on the way home while I ride in style?"

"Dinner time? I never got lunch! I don't have enough energy to give you a ride home." I groaned. It was all just for show. I was still a little full from breakfast and not at all unhappy about losing the bet. Both of us had made progress on what we needed to do. I turned to Mercedes.

"Thanks for your help. I'll see you tomorrow morning."
"You'll see me before that," she answered with a cryptic smile.

Chapter Eleven
Larry
July 18

"Here she is! I found her!" Shine clutched the porch railing as she hopped up and down, pointing at me as I vaulted the chain link fence. I waded through a whirlpool of dogs, stopping to pat one head, then another.

Maureen came out on the porch, wiping her hands on her apron. "Where've you been? Shine and I have been back for hours."

"Library. Working on my lost horse poster."

Maureen raised an eyebrow. "You got that sweaty just coming home from the library? It's all downhill."

I grinned. "Maybe. But I pumped the pedals the whole time anyway. I think I set a land speed record."

Maureen rolled her eyes. "You don't have a bike. Were you with that Montoya boy? Well, anyway, I'm glad you're home. I was getting worried. Feed the critters for me, will you? Your mom says she's bringing a guest to dinner, and Dutch invited Mercedes. I want everything ready for them."

My heart leaped in my chest. Was my mother's guest Dad? I filled all the dog bowls, then went into the laundry room and filled the cat bowls while Shine set the table.

"Mom's home! I'll get the gate!" Shine shrieked. She exploded through the front door, leaving the screen to slam behind her. I went to the front window and watched my mother's Volvo slowly part the sea of dogs. Before Shine could close the gate, a red Corvette followed. My heart dropped in my chest. Dad wouldn't be caught dead in a red Corvette. He was more a beat-up Dodge truck kind of guy.

The man who climbed out of the fancy car looked a little too slick, his hair and mustache too groomed. Muscles, the kind of pecs and abs a man gets by working out at some expensive gym instead of working hard, bulged under his mauve polo shirt. The pointy-toed cowboy boots that peeked out beneath his khakis looked like they'd never gotten dusty or been in a stirrup. My dad's round-toed work boots were so worn that the steel caps shone through the busted-up leather. He leaned back into the car and brought out a bottle of wine. I heard a kerfluffle of dogs at the gate and looked up to see Mercedes slip through. I was surprised to find her walking.

Dutch came up behind me and put a hand on my shoulder. "Well, come on, Girly-girl. We might as well meet our guests. And put on a friendly face, will you?"

"Who is he? And what are you doing home this time of day? Aren't you supposed to be at work?" I asked. Before Dutch could answer, Maureen came out of the kitchen and hustled us all onto the porch. Shine, looking more sober and shy than usual, climbed the stairs and took Maureen's hand.

"Girls," my mother said as she slipped her hand under the man's elbow and leaned into him, "this is Larry. You know, my co-worker? He brought down all my files and papers today. This is Maureen, my big sister. And her friend Dutch. And my girls: Margaret, but we call her Punkin, and Sadie, who we call Sunshine." Mom's face glowed as she jerked her chin at each of us in turn. The way she leaned into Larry didn't look at all like how two co-workers should interact.

"And this is Mercedes Escudero, the head librarian," Dutch said as Mercedes joined the group.

Larry's face split into a too-toothy grin. He stepped forward, hand out, repeating names as he shook each of our hands. His hand was warm and smooth, his grip firm. I felt like I was being interviewed for a job I didn't want.

"You must be called Punkin because of that red hair of yours," he said, trying way too hard to make friends with me.

"Nope. It's because I'm fat and have a wicked smile." I grinned diabolically, trying to look like Vincent Price in *House of Wax*. Or maybe Jack Nicholson in *One Flew Over the Cuckoo's Nest.* Everyone around me stiffened except Mercedes, whose own smile looked even more wicked than mine.

"Punk," Maureen warned, her voice low.

My mother's mouth smiled, but her eyes narrowed with anger. "Well, now. Let's go in and eat, shall we?" She and Larry stepped onto the porch. He handed the bottle of wine to Maureen.

"Thank you for inviting me," he said.

Maureen nodded and frowned at the bottle. "We don't have wine glasses in this house. You'll have to drink this out of a juice glass."

"Just like they do in France," Larry said as we all trooped in the front door.

"Mercedes? Want some?" Dutch asked, holding up the bottle.

"No thanks. I know the house rules," Mercedes said, giving me a wink. Dutch got down a couple of little glasses, the kind that came filled with cheese spread from the supermarket as Larry pulled a corkscrew from his pocket. What kind of man carries a corkscrew around in his pocket? Larry poured one and held it out to Dutch, who waved him off.

"We don't drink," she said. "House rules. But you go ahead."

"You shoulda been to the zoo with me and Dutch! We saw lots and lots of aminals," Shine said when we were all seated. I winced at her little girl words. She knew better, but when she wanted to be cute, she always reverted. As Shine went on and on about the 'elipants and the whinos,' I slumped in my seat and studied Larry from under furrowed brows. Everyone tried to make conversation, asking each other questions about their interests and their day. I didn't listen to much of it.

"Mother," I said when the conversation had died down, "have you got any pictures of Wildfire on your phone?"

My mother looked so relieved that I'd said anything at all that I thought she was going to burst out in tears. She smiled, tight-lipped while she chewed her mouthful of food, swallowed, and patted her napkin against her mouth. "I don't think so, Punkin. Why do you ask?"

I shoved a big broccoli tree into my mouth before answering. "It's for a notice I'm putting up. A missing horse notice. On this website. It's called *Netposse: Missing, Lost, Stolen Pet Database.* It'll get shared with horse auctions and rodeos all across America. Mercedes is helping me build the page." I looked at Mercedes, who was staring intently at Larry, her lips tight in what I thought was a disgusted sneer.

Larry wrinkled his forehead and frowned in a way that I assumed was an attempt at looking sympathetic, but only looked pathetic. "You've lost your horse?"

"I guess my mother hasn't had time to fill you in on our lives," I muttered, then shoved in another forkful of broccoli while I watched my mother twitch.

Dutch smiled. "So Mercedes is helping you, after all!"

I winced, hoping that Dutch hadn't shared that I'd called the librarian another high and mighty professional who thought too highly of herself.

"Yes. Us women need to support each other." Mercedes said, glancing over at Larry. I think she was hinting that he wasn't welcome or needed, but he just smiled back at her. I think her comment went over his head. And I thought scientists were smart.

"I've got a picture." Maureen slid her chair back and left the table. When she returned, she had a framed picture in her hand. She handed it to Dutch, who smiled at it, then passed it to my mother, who passed it to Larry, then to Shine, and then to Mercedes, making its way around the whole table before it finally got to me. Everyone smiled and ooohed and ahhed when they looked at it, raising my hopes, but when it was finally my turn to see it, I frowned.

"Nope. This won't do. I'm on Wildfire's back, and he's saddled. What I need is one with just Wildfire, so people can see his complete conformation."

"Oh, that's right," Mercedes said, frowning. "Makes him easier to identify."

"Maybe I'll ask Dad," I said, and watched Larry frown.

My mother stiffened. "Oh, sweetie. I wouldn't bother your father with this. He's busy with . . . other things. And you know as well as I do that all the pictures burned up in the fire."

"What about the boxes you packed? They're still in temporary storage, right? And maybe he has some on his phone?" My questions went unanswered. After another stiff moment, everyone returned to eating.

When I thought it was safe to do so, I pushed back my chair, thanked Maureen for the meal, and excused myself. I said I wanted to walk around the block to settle my stomach. No one argued. I think they were just as happy to get rid of me, the troublemaker, as I was to escape their company.

I was halfway to the gate when I heard someone come out on the porch behind me. "Margaret?"

I turned and saw Mercedes leaning against a pillar. "What? And why are you calling me Margaret?"

Mercedes stepped down and crossed the yard to me. She stood close enough that I could smell the jungle-y flowers of her perfume. "Punkin is too cutesy for a young woman who wants to be taken seriously. And Punk sounds too thuggish. You're a Margaret to me: strong and capable."

I sighed. "I don't feel either strong or capable right now."

I know," she said, nodding her head. "But things will get better. I promise."

I wanted to ask how she could possibly know that, but I couldn't bring myself to say it. It was too snarky, and Mercedes didn't deserve that. I nodded and went out the gate, watching out of the corner of my eye until Mercedes had gone back inside.

The sun had already set, and twilight lingered pink and peach in the sky. Light seeped under Paco's garage door, so I went over and stuck my foot into the crack between the door and the cement before I knocked. The sound was a little less booming that way.

"¿Que te pasa? It's me, the calabaza head," I said.

Paco pulled the door up. "One thing you are not is a calabaza head. You are one smart Chica." He frowned, those clear, light greenish gray eyes of his studying my face. "What'szup? You look sad or mad or something."

I dropped down on the concrete stoop, where I had sat before to tell Paco about the fire. "My mother brought a guy to dinner tonight. This guy, this Larry is supposed to be a co-worker. A scientist, like my mother! All grown up, and stuff. But he's acting all syrupy sweet. And you should see the eyes my mother makes at him. I think they've got something going between them, and it makes me sick to my stomach. If he comes back again, I'm leaving."

Paco looked up from the wheel he was balancing. "Leaving?"

"Yeah. Leaving. I'll go back to my dad, or I'll just run away. I can't be around that guy. He makes my stomach churn."

Paco shook his head. "You wan' maybe I beat him up for you or something?"

I laughed. "I don't think that would do any good. But thanks for the offer."

"I'm working on a present for you. It won' do any good, either, but come back tomorrow morning and it'll be ready."

"A present? For me? Why?" I asked.

Paco smiled and shrugged. "Because you're my friend. And because maybe you need something to go a little right in your life right now. So go home, so I can work on it."

I got up, and I left, but I didn't go home. I walked around the neighborhood until a red Corvette rumbled by in the dark. When I got home, my mother, Mercedes, Maureen, and Dutch were hunkered over the never-ending Monopoly game that was the reason we could never eat in the dinning room. I waved at then, then slipped into my bedroom before they could talk with me. I lay awake, staring at the ceiling and listening to make sure that the Corvette didn't come back.

Chapter Twelve
Wildfire II
July 19

"You sure you don't want to come with us? I don't think you've ever seen the Balloon Museum," Maureen said when we were seated at the table for breakfast.

"Yeah, I'm sure," I answered. "I really have to finish off my lost horse page. The longer I wait, the less likely I get Wildfire back. The website says so."

"I can drop you off at the library on our way out."

I shook my head. "You don't have to do that. It's a short walk."

"How about picking you up for lunch? The middle of the day can get pretty hot."

Again, I shook my head. I tried to look like I wasn't bothered by Maureen's line of questions. It was almost as if she knew I had plans to see Paco and she wanted me to confess them. But I wasn't going to do that. She and Dutch had said Paco was trouble. How could I explain that he was the best friend I'd had in a long time? "I don't know how long it'll take me to get this page up and running. I'll come home when I'm finished. I promise. If I had a phone, I could call you when I was done."

Maureen put up her hands, deflecting my comment. "That's something you'll have to take up with your mother. She's had a lot of things on her mind. I'm sure she's just forgotten about the phone. But I'm glad you're going to see Mercedes. I'm sure you and she will have a lot to talk about."

"Mom can't forget about Punk's phone. Not the way Punk's been whining about it. How could anybody forget?" Shine said. I glared at her to let her know her remarks weren't appreciated.

I closed the gate for Maureen and Shine, waving at the car until it turned the corner, then I walked over to Paco's garage.

"Trick or treat," I said, rapping on the door.

"Close your eyes," he said. "They closed?"

I nodded my head.

"They closed?" he said again, and I realized that, standing on the other side of the door, he couldn't see me nod.

"Yes. They're closed,"

The garage door rumbled up. "Bueno. Open them."

A bike stood in the middle of his garage. It was a girl's ten speed, and it was painted dark brown. Black streamers hung off the ends of the handlebars, and orange and yellow flames surrounded the words 'Wildfire II' that were painted in old English letters along the top tube of the frame.

Paco scuffed his sneaker on the concrete. "I know it's not the Wildfire you want, but it's the best I can do."

I choked back both the laugh and the sob that fought to rise up my throat. "This is so cool! Where'd you find a bike named Wildfire?"

Paco shook his head. "I didn't find it. I made it. I make a little money fixing up old bikes. A friend of mine sells them at the flea market. But this one, I fixed up for you."

I fingered the streamers. They were made of a supple leather.

"They make those for motorcycles. But they kind of look like a mane, no?" The pride in Paco's eyes made my heart swell.

"This is very special. Thank you," I said, squeezing the words past a lump in my throat.

Paco jerked his chin towards the front yard. "Try it out. Let's ride."

We rode to the library and walked in, red-cheeked and smiling. Mercedes looked up from the help desk and smiled back as we walked back to the computer area. I worked on the story for my missing horse page while Paco worked on his online class. I was close to finished when

I smelled fruit and flowers and knew that Mercedes was standing behind me.

"Well? What do you think?" I asked.

"Looks pretty good," she answered. "The interlibrary loan copy of *Horse Theft. Been There—Done That* showed up yesterday afternoon, after you'd gone home. I read it last night. You know that sheriff you were working with back at home? It suggests you use him as the contact instead of you."

"Why?" Deputy Chavez had been less than helpful when I was in Alamitos. I saw no reason in getting him involved again now.

"Apparently there are plenty of scammers, thieves and fraudsters out there. Some are so shameless that they prey on people in crisis. Especially women like us. We tend to be more emotional and more trusting."

"Tell me about it," I muttered, remembering how easy it had been for Trudy Goodheart to convince me to hand over Wildfire.

"They study sites like this, then email, suggesting they have information but they need money to provide it. Or they suggest they meet you, and then they steal your car or hold you up at gunpoint."

"Creeps," I said, almost spitting the word out.

"That's a nice word for them. Anyway, the book suggests that those kinds of people won't contact law enforcement, and if they do, the sheriff will be able to deal with them better than you can."

"Good idea." I began typing in the phone number for Ernesto Chavez, the deputy sheriff who was handling my case. Mercedes made a little *ahem* sound that let me know that she didn't think I should be doing that. "What?" I asked, fingers poised over the keyboard.

"Maybe you should talk with him before you put his contact information on the internet. At least give him a heads up so he won't be surprised when people start calling him. And I wanted to show you these, in case one works for you." Mercedes pulled up a chair and sat down next to me. She held out her phone, displaying the faces of a bay and a brown and white paint. Behind them, I saw an adobe stable with blue gates and trim.

"These are my equine babies: Galadriel and Navajo. Does Galadriel look close enough like Wildfire that you can use her picture?"

I shook my head. "Wildfire doesn't have a star like your Galadriel. And his muzzle is darker and his head is broader. Besides, the website suggested I post a full body picture."

"That I have." Mercedes swiped through a dozen more pictures of her horses. They were of no use to me, but I could tell that sharing them made her happy, so I sat quietly and let her show me. "You know, you should come by, visit the horses. Maybe it'd make you feel better to be around them. I live down on the end of Candelaria Road, right near the Nature Center. It's walking distance from the library, and your aunt's house is halfway in between."

I shook my head. "I'm not ready for that. Other horses make me feel sad. I checked with Dutch and Maureen and my mother. None of them have pictures of Wildfire. Can I use your phone to call my dad and ask if he has pictures?"

Mercedes handed the phone to me. "Sure. And call that sheriff, too. Hearing from you might get him going on the case again. Why don't you use one of the conference rooms so you don't have to whisper?"

She pointed to the little, glass-walled rooms that study groups use, then went back to the help desk. I called Deputy Chavez, who took a long time to remember me and my case, but promised to check the website once I'd gotten everything posted, and to call me at Maureen's house if he got any leads. I called my dad next.

My fingers shook. I hadn't talked to my dad in the four days since my mother brought us down to Maureen's. How would he be, living all alone? A bigger mess than when we'd left? Had he eaten? Cleaned the place up? Gotten his act together? Or had he fallen even deeper into the lethargy that had pulled him away from us?

"What?!" Dad's voice sounded so angry when he answered that I almost hung up.

"Dad?"

There was a long silence. "Punk? Is that you? This isn't your phone number. Caller ID didn't recognize you so I figured you were yet another of those irritating scammers."

"Of course it's not my phone," I said. "I lost my phone. In the fire. Remember? Mercedes the librarian let me use her phone."

"The librarian? What librarian?"

"I told you. Her name's Mercedes. She's been helping me search for Wildfire," I said.

Again, there was a long pause. "What library are you at?"

"The one near Maureen and Dutch's house."

"Uhm," Dad said. I could almost hear the gears turning in his head as he processed this. "You're at Maureen and Dutch's house?"

"Yeah," I answered. "Didn't you know?"

My dad gave a long sigh. I could see him in my mind's eye, stroking down his beard the way he does when he's thinking through a difficult question. "I came back to an empty house. I had no idea where you all had gone. I called your mother, but she didn't pick up. I called Maureen and Dutch. Left messages. They haven't returned my calls, either. Every time the phone rings, I rush to answer it. For the last four days, it's been nothing but people trying to get me to send them money. Scammers hoping I've gotten the insurance settlement."

"You've just been sitting there, waiting for us to call?" I could see my dad, sitting half buried in laundry, some odd show on the TV in front of him. It made my heart ache.

"Well, no. I've put away the laundry. And washed the dishes. Most of them, anyway. And I've talked with a counselor about getting some help for my . . . inability to act."

"Wow! That's a lot," I said, then instantly regretted it. I didn't want Dad to think I was criticizing how little he'd been doing before we left.

"Yeah, well I guess your mother got to a breaking point, and so did I. I still feel a bit hopeless, but lying around doing nothing wasn't helping. I can get out. It's not like the phone's chained to the wall here or anything."

"Like in the old days," I said, remembering all the old movies with phones that were attached to cords. "Maybe that's how you should answer those unidentified callers: with 'Sam Spade Detective Agency.'"

"Then they'd think I was a detective. Either that, or I was crazy. Either way, they'd think that calling me was a bad move."

I let out a sigh of relief. If my dad still had his sense of humor and was thinking of old movies, things couldn't be completely out of whack. "Well, Dad, that's why I called. I'm working on my own little detective thing. I'm filling out a missing horse report. After the fire, things were in such chaos that we didn't do all the things we should have done to find Wildfire. Since I've been down here, I've been studying up on how to report a missing horse. I need a picture of Wildfire. Do you have one on your phone that you can send to me?"

"Yeah, I've got some pictures," Dad said. "I'll send them to your mom's phone. Better yet, I'll come down. Your mother and I need to have a face-to-face talk."

"Good! Come for dinner. But, can you send the pictures to this phone now? So I can work with them? I'm trying to get them posted on a website. And then I'm going to create a poster that Deputy Chavez says he'll distribute to all the other sheriff's posses, and at rodeos and horse auctions."

"I'm on it. See you soon, Punk. And, I love you." Dad hung up before I could tell him that I loved him, too. Seconds later, Mercedes' phone started pinging. I walked over to the help desk and handed it to her.

"You made two calls: to your dad, and to a sheriff? What was his name? You mind if I keep both in my phone as contacts, so I can help out? At least until you get a phone?"

"Sure," I responded. "But Ernesto Chavez is a sheriff's deputy, not the sheriff himself. And my dad just forwarded a bunch of pictures to you. Can we look through them? Decide which to put on the website and poster?"

Mercedes' thumbs danced across her phone's keyboard. "Er-nest-o-Chavez. Got it. Got your dad, too. Here's the pics." She scrolled through the pictures as I looked over her shoulder. Dad had sent a dozen pictures, and two were just perfect. One was a summer picture and the other a winter, even, so people could see the differences in Wildfire's coat. "You're right. Your Wildfire doesn't look anything like my Galadriel. Horses are just as individual as people once you get to know them. Tell you what: I'll log onto my email account on the computer you're using, then download these two pictures to the desktop so you can use them."

"Great," I said. "I'll let you know when I'm done. Could you text Deputy Chavez the website's URL so he can get going on the things he was going to do?"

"You bet!" Mercedes said. "Oh, and I wanted to tell you: after you went to bed, your mom and I had a long talk about how us women should stand on our own two feet. About how we shouldn't rely on men to make us happy. Not sure if she's ready to hear it, but I wanted you to know." She pointed one of those perfectly manicured fingers at me. "Us women have to take care of each other. You need to talk, come see me, ok?"

"Okay!" I walked back to the computer area feeling stronger and more confident than I had at any time since the fire. I finally had an adult ally, and I was doing something about Wildfire! I had the sense that I'd helped dad, too. Maybe things were finally beginning to work themselves out and life would return to normal.

Chapter Thirteen
The Gritty Truth
July 19

I'd just finished both the webpage and the downloadable poster and was reading through them again, checking for errors when Paco scooted back his chair. "Man, Chica; this math stuff is mind-numbing. I gotta take a break. Let's get some lunch."

"Sure," I said, "but I don't have any money. How about we go root through Maureen's fridge?"

Paco shook his head. "Na. I got something else in mind. Come on."

I went to the help desk, where Mercedes looked up, shaking her head to get her dangly earrings away from her face. "Success?"

"Yeah, I think so," I answered. "I didn't log out, left the website up on the screen. You think you could take a look at it?"

Mercedes nodded. "As soon as Naomi takes over the help desk, I'll grab my lunch and eat it while checking it out."

"No way, Ms. Escudero," Paco said. "The sign says *No Food at the Computers*. You gonna break that rule?"

Mercedes smiled at Paco. "Yep. That's me. Rule breaking rebel. You two going out for lunch? I'll talk to you when you get back." Mercedes waved us off, and we walked outside into a wall of dry heat that felt like an oven. Cicadas buzzed in the elm trees. Kids shrieked in the public pool. Traffic rumbled by on a street that wavered in the heat.

"Hey, Chica. Go stand over there in the shade and watch this." Paco pointed to a place near the bike stand, then strode off to the pool entrance, where a bored-looking blond girl in a lifeguard tank top leaned on her hand inside the window.

"Hey," Paco said to the girl, "I'm not going to swim. I just gotta pick up my cousin. He was supposed to come home for lunch."

The girl didn't answer. She waved her hand lazily and Paco disappeared through the door into the boy's locker room. A few minutes later, he came back out.

"What was that all about?" I asked as Paco moved the rings of numbers on the lock that secured our two bikes to the rack.

"I just wanted to show you how to get in without paying. The pool's toilets beat going behind a bush in the park. And there's always towels laying around, and little, half used bottles of shampoo."

"And I need to know this because?"

Paco climbed onto his bike and pushed off. "You're the one who keeps saying she's going to run away, Chica. I just want you to know a few tricks."

We rode south along the sidewalk, cars rushing past and bathing us in waves of hot air. The distance shimmered like a mirage. We had gone a couple of miles when we came to a sign that had a picture of a cow sitting in a basket. Paco turned off the sidewalk and onto the asphalt of the old, drive-up restaurant. A few cars huddled in the shade under the long, metal roofs that skirted each side of the run-down building. As Paco was locking up our bikes, a girl carrying a tray backed out the door. The smell of beef and grease as she passed by made me weak in the knees.

Paco held the door open for me and we entered a dinning room that was almost as hot as outside. Flies beat themselves against windows that probably hadn't been cleaned since poodle skirts were in fashion. Paco slipped onto the red vinyl bench of a booth. I did the same. My thighs stuck to it. Above the kitchen door, a TV soundlessly presented the noon edition of the local news.

"Hey, Doll. Haven't seen you in here in quite a while." The woman looked over the top of her half glasses at us. I couldn't help but stare at her red hair. It was piled so high on her head that I thought she'd have trouble making it through doors.

"Hey, Sal. Yeah. Things've been good." Paco jerked his chin towards me. "I want you to meet my friend, Chica. We want the Sal special."

Sal rolled her eyes, gave a sigh, and put her fist on her hip. "Well, ain't you the big spender."

"I'm teaching Chica a thing or two today," Paco said.

Sal shook her head and looked at me. "Keep yourself out of trouble, Doll, and you won't need to know anything this punk can teach you. But seriously: if it gets bad – I mean real bad, come see me. I got a heart for kids like you, and I don't want to see you hurt. Got it?"

"Got it." I nodded solemnly, and Sal went back into the kitchen, where someone was playing *Kings and Liars* so loud that the walls shook. I turned to Paco as soon as the door was shut, muting the noise.

"What was that all about?"

Paco shrugged. "Just what she said, Chica. You need help, come see Sal. But don't do it unless, you know, you can't figure any other way out. She's a last resort."

"Okaaaay," I said, frowning. I was still trying to process what Paco was doing when Sal came back out and set down two plastic baskets of food.

"This one has mayo and it wasn't supposed to, and this one has pickles. And when they said they wanted Coke, they really meant Pepsi. Enjoy." Sal set the baskets in front of us. The paper cups looked like they'd been left on the counter too long.

"Did we order this?" I asked.

Sal laughed. "No, Doll. You didn't. And neither did the customer. That's why you get them." She disappeared back into the kitchen while I watched Paco suppress a laugh.

"That's the Sal special," he said when he could control himself. "Whenever the kitchen gets an order wrong, or the customer changes his mind, Sal puts the food aside instead of throwing it away. She gives it to whoever shows up and asks for it. At the end of the night, she bags it up before she puts it, real careful like, in the dumpster so it don't fall over. You need food, go to a restaurant and check the dumpster, or look for bags on top of trash cans. Sal's not the only one who doesn't want to waste food."

I nodded and picked up my burger. It was soggy, and the fries were so limp it was like trying to pick up spaghetti, but they still tasted good if I doused them in katsup. The Coke was completely flat and watered down from, I figured, melted ice. We ate our food, then wiped down all the tables and threw away all the wrappers and napkins littering the floor before we left. Sal never came out to check on us.

"Okay, you've taught me how to find a toilet and shower, and where to get free food. What else is on your agenda?" I asked when we were again riding south. We came to where the road crossed over the freeway. Paco pointed to a run-down hotel.

"Another good place to get a shower. Hang out here early in the morning. Lots of people don't close the door when they check out. You can slip in and take a shower in style. Just make sure they took their stuff with them when they go, so they don't come back and surprise you."

"Isn't that illegal?" I asked.

Paco looked at me, his brows low over his eyes as if he couldn't believe I'd asked that. "Chica, I think it's illegal to run away. If you're going to do that, might as well break a couple more laws."

We rode over the freeway, the cars whooshing by beneath us. A giant concrete arroyo ran down the center, separating the traffic going east from the traffic going west. Paco pointed down. "Up on the edges, right under the roadway, there's a place where the concrete flattens out. It's kind of hidden and it's protected from the rain. Good place to spend the night, but make sure there's no one else there, Chica. You don't want to share your spot with nobody else."

I studied the chain-link fences along the bridge and the sides of the freeway. "How do I get there?"

Paco nodded. "I'll show you."

On the other side of the freeway, we turned off the main road and into a neighborhood. In the center of it, an empty park dozed in the afternoon heat. The ground in the corner of the park sloped down to a giant metal tube. It was slightly shorter than me, and corrugated, the bottom covered with sand. "That's it," he said.

I stared at the tube and the darkness within it. "That's what?"

"How to get to the freeway." He walked in, and I reluctantly followed. When we were deep into the dark, Paco leaned his bike against the side and took my hand. I followed him down the slope, clutching at him with one hand while the other trailed along the bumpy wall. We hadn't taken more than a dozen steps before I saw a dim circle of light ahead. The circle got bigger until I realized that it was the end of the tube. We were halfway to it when another tube broke off from it, sloping up. We took the second tube and found ourselves at the edge of the freeway, with cars zipping past us, filling the tube with noise. Paco leaned out and twisted, looking up and over our shoulders. "There, Chica. See it?" I followed his gaze and saw the place he was talking about: a little concrete platform hidden from view by the overhanging streets. "Of course, if you don't wanna sleep here, there's always bushes and stuff, especially down near the Rio. It gets way harder when winter comes. Come on," he said. "Let's get our bikes. I got one more thing to show you."

We rode south until we got within sight of Central Avenue. Paco rode around the edge of the one, lone skyscraper and stopped in the shade. I pulled up next to him, wondering what he was going to teach me here. Central Avenue is not the kind of street a kid wants to hang out on. It used to be Route 66, my dad once told me, and it has that run-down, seedy look of a place that used to be grand, but got forgotten in time. An old motel sat across the street from the skyscraper. Men in stained t-shirts sat on folding chairs in the parking lot, drinking beer and smoking cigarettes. A couple of women leaned against the posts of the motel's sign, which depicted a cowboy throwing a lariat, the paint faded and flaking.

Paco leaned into me, whispering. "See that lady over there? The one with the big platform shoes?"

I focused on the women. The one that Paco was talking about wore a miniskirt that looked dirty, even from across four lanes of traffic. Her shirt was tight and short, exposing a slim midriff. Her hair was teased, and her bangs looked like they'd been rolled over orange juice cans. The other woman said something to her, and she smiled, exposing bad teeth and empty places where teeth should be.

"So?" My stomach tightened as I waited for him to say more.

"That woman? That's mi madre. My mother."

I felt like I'd been slapped in the face. I turned and stared at Paco. "What?"

"Come on. I'll explain while we're riding." Paco backed his bike farther into the shadows, then turned around and pedaled away. I followed, my heart pounding even though we had just stopped.

"I don't understand," I said once I'd caught up with him. "I thought Lluvia was your mother."

Paco shook his head. "She's my aunt. My father's sister."

"And your father's . . ."

"In jail." Paco stood on the pedals. I had to push hard to keep up.

"Chica, I wanted you to see. You think things are bad at your house. But they can be worse. Way worse. So now, if you still feel you have to leave, go ahead and do it. It's not going to be nice. You're going to be scared and hungry and cold. Better you go home and work it out with your mother. She's not as bad as you think she is."

I pressed my lips together, holding back a thousand questions and a lot of sadness. I couldn't believe Paco lived with this, every day. I felt ashamed that I'd felt so bad for myself. He was right: things could be a lot worse.

When we turned the corner onto our street, Paco slammed on his brakes and skidded to a stop so quickly that I ended up several feet in front of him. Straddling my bike, I walked backwards. The pedals banged against my shins. "What?" I ask.

Paco's face had gone pale. He jutted his chin towards his house. I turned and saw a couple of police cars parked in front. Several men stood at the front door, talking to Lluvia.

"Chica," Paco said, his voice low and serious, "Turn around. Now. Don' come back till dinner time. I don't want you mixed up in this."

"Mixed up in what?" I asked. "Where will I go?"

Paco shrugged. "Anywhere but here. Go to the library. Check in with Mercedes. Ride around the park. Just make sure all those cars are gone before you come back. I knew this would happen sooner or later. Time to face it." He gave a sigh and slowly rode towards the police. One of them saw him. The policeman left the front stoop and began walking towards Paco. Heart pounding, I rode in a tight circle and raced down the street.

Chapter Fourteen
The Get Away
July 19

I rode downhill, standing on the pedals. When I got to a big street, I turned left and rode until I came to a stoplight. The street sign said *Candelaria*, which sounded familiar although I didn't know why. I crossed the street and continued downhill on Candelaria, sitting on the seat and letting gravity pull me down the sidewalk. The river must be at the bottom of this slope somewhere: maybe a mile ahead? Or two? I didn't know, but I didn't think I could get lost. Albuquerque is a giant grid of streets set on a slope between the Sandia Mountains and the Rio Grande. That makes navigating it easy.

I wished other parts of my life were so easy to navigate. I still didn't understand how someone could be so cruel as to steal a horse from a girl who's lost everything. Or how a family can blow apart at the time when they most need to stick together. Or how Paco could be such a nice guy when his parents were so messed up. I passed under a freeway and through a couple more lights. The road became rural. The sidewalks disappeared. Big cottonwood trees leaned over the road, making a cool, green tunnel for me to ride through. I thought I must be coming close to the river. I closed my eyes and listened to the steady click of the bike as it rolled along. When I opened them again, it was because I heard a droning sound.

A bomber.

Again.

It started out as a low, dull background sound but built until it filled my head with its throbbing. My front wheel wobbled as I tried to catch a sight of it through the cottonwoods. It passed almost overhead, its orange belly flashing through the canopy of leaves. I could have thrown a rock and hit it.

Enough, I told myself. It is time to go home. I pushed on the right handlebar and the bike entered a lazy arc. I was halfway through my turn when I saw blue gates and trim on an adobe stable, and I remembered where I heard the name Candelaria Road before. These were the same blue gates I'd seen in Mercedes' pictures of her horses. I remembered her saying that I could talk with her about anything, and she knew Paco already. Would she talk with me about him? Help me understand what he was going through? I put my hand on the gate, then pulled it back, unsure what to say. Maybe it'd be better if I just went home.

I remember Mercedes saying that her house wasn't too far from the library, and she's right. It's only three or four miles, but it's all uphill. I went so slow, I had to stand on the pedals a lot to keep myself from wobbling. I was more than halfway home when I heard a rumble behind me. This time, the rumble wasn't a bomber, and it wasn't traffic. I looked over my shoulder at a huge thunder head building itself up and up into the sky. Its upper reaches were white and billowy and looked like cauliflower, but its belly was dark. Ominous. It flashed – not lightning I could see, but lightening deep inside the cloud. A moment later, the cloud rumbled again. I gasped. I had forgotten to count to see how far away the cloud was, but I was sure the time between the flash and rumble was short. Too short.

I turned and stepped hard on the pedals. I was glad the monsoons were finally here. We needed the water to stop all the wildfires. But I didn't want to be caught out in it. Monsoons could be violent, with whipping winds that could throw me right off my bike, and lightning strikes that've been known to set the tops of trees on fire. And hailstones, sometimes as big as golf balls. Get hit by one of those and you could have your skull split. The cloud roiled and built behind me, blotting out the sun and throwing the road into an eerie twilight. I raced it home, trying to make it back to the safety of Maureen's porch before it overtook me.

And I won, skidding to a stop long enough to open the gate, then running alongside my bike as the first fat raindrops splattered around me. I laughed with the sheer audacity of it. I had raced the storm. And won. I leaned Wildfire II against the railings and hopped onto the porch.

Dutch exploded through the screen door and threw her arms around me, hugging me tightly to her. "Oh, Girly Girl! You had us worried sick! Where've you been?"

"Just riding!" I said, laughing at how good it felt to finally win at something, even something so trivial as beating the storm.

Dutch let out a long breath and I feel her relax. "When all those cops showed up next door, we didn't know what to think. But here you are, safe and sound. Why didn't you call?"

I felt the laughter escape from me, like air from a balloon. In my race against the storm, I'd forgotten about Paco and his problems. "No phone," I reminded her for what must have been the twenty-umph time. "Dutch, what happened next door? Was there a break in or something? Is Lluvia ok?"

Dutch dropped onto the porch swing, patting the seat next to her for me to join her. The dozen or so dogs who'd been looking through the screen took it as an invitation for them, too, and they pushed the door open and poured onto the porch, butts and tails wagging in joy over seeing me again. I patted one head after another as they jockeyed to get close to me.

"Lluvia's fine. And no break in. It's that no good nephew of hers."

"Paco?" I asked, incredulously.

"Paco," Dutch replied, saying the word as if it were a curse. "He and a friend have been stealing bikes, grinding off their ID numbers, changing out handlebars and seats and repainting them, then selling them at the flea market. It was quite a racket. The friend got caught and fingered Lluvia's nephew. Now he's right back in juvie, where he'd been until Lluvia convinced CYFD that she could keep him on the straight and narrow. That boy's such a disappointment. This, after all she did for him." She shook her head, clucking softly to herself. My throat knotted with emotion as I looked at the hail stones bouncing off Wildfire II, pinging so loudly that I was having trouble catching Dutch's words.

Waves of guilt and anger washed over me. My cheeks burned. Somewhere in this city, a girl was missing her bike, and here it was, with me. How was I going to figure out how to return it?

"He seemed so nice," I said weakly.

Dutch snorted. "Appearances can be deceiving. That woman who stole your horse, she seemed nice at the time, too."

"No," I said, jumping to my feet. "There's a difference! This Trudy Goodheart, she's a real criminal! Paco? He's . . . well, he's . . . "

"A criminal, too. Whatever excuses you make for him, whatever problems he's had, he's still made a bad decision."

"But he was willing to face it," I said. "He could have ridden away with me. He could have hidden somewhere. Instead, he told me to ride away, to keep me out of it. Then he rode to the house. He faced the consequences."

Dutch sat still a long time, thinking about it. "Well, it's a start. Maybe he's ready to turn over a new leaf. Let's get supper ready. Your mother is bringing back that man again for dinner." The way she spat out *that man* let me know exactly what Dutch thought about Larry. We climbed off the porch swing and herded the dogs into the house.

I'd set the table when my mother and her coworker ran through the front door. They laughed as they wiped the rain from their faces. My mother's hair was plastered to her forehead. Her silk blouse was plastered to her bra. It looked like the two of them had gone swimming fully clothed, but all they'd done was run from their cars into the house. The rain beat a steady tattoo on the roof that sounded like a 100-piece drum corps was up there.

"Well! That was refreshing!" My mother shouted over the pounding rain.

"You look like a drowned rat. Maybe you should go change," I shouted back. My mother's face darkened, and I was sure she was going to say something mean, right there in front of that Larry guy. I preempted her. "Sorry," I muttered. "You don't look like a drowned rat. You look like a drowned . . . uhm . . . scientist?"

My mother laughed. "That's closer to the truth. When it rains, it pours! Let me change." Her heels tippity-tapped down the hall. When she came back, she wore a sweatshirt and a pair of leggings and her hair is in a high ponytail that would have been swingy if it wasn't so wet.

"What a day!" Shine said as we took our places around the table. "Me an' Aunty Maureen went to the Bawoon Museum, and when we got back, there were powice cars all over the street and Punk was missing."

"Really?" My mother's head swiveled and she caught me in her death stare. "Punkin? What did you do?"

"Nothing!" I stuffed half a roll in my mouth so I couldn't answer, then pointed at it as I chewed. It wasn't going to buy me much time, but I'd hoped I could come up with something that made sense and didn't make everyone mad at me. I was chewing when the rain suddenly stopped. It was pounding one minute and the next it had stopped completely, like a light switch was flipped or something. It's another thing that makes monsoon season so strange.

I took a deep breath through my nose and let it out in a whoosh, glad the pounding was over.

I didn't realize that the end of the rain was the calm before the storm.

Before I swallowed, the gate squeaked. The dogs exploded into barks and bays as a pickup rumbled into the yard.

"Dadeeeeee!" Shine pushed back her chair so quickly that it clattered over backward. She rushed out the front door and launched herself off the porch, wrapping her legs around Dad's waist and attaching herself like a tick. Dad was clean shaven, and his hair was trimmed. He looked pale and thin, and a little shaky, but oh, so good. He put his nose on the top of Shine's head and breathed in her scent as if she were a rare perfume.

"How's my baby?" He asked.

"Oh, Daddy! I've missed you so much! Are you going to move in with us here, too? We can all go to the zoo and museum and the pool every weekend! It'll be so much fun!" Shine's little girl accent was gone. I guessed she doesn't need it around Dad.

"What are you doing here, Curtis?" My mother's voice was sharp. I turned and saw her standing just back of the door. Larry had a protective arm around her shoulders. I wanted to bite it. Dad beamed at his wife. I didn't know if he couldn't see what Larry was doing because she was back in the shadows, or if he was choosing not to make an issue of it.

"Seeing my girls. All three of them. You look well, Elaine."

My mother let out a little, indignant sniff. "You should have called first, so I'd be prepared."

"Sorry if this is sudden. Punk asked for pictures of Wildfire, and I figured the sooner I got them to her, the better."

My mother glared at me. "You have pictures for Punk?"

I shrugged. "When you said you didn't have any, I told you I'd try Dad."

Dad took a lumbering step toward the house. It wasn't easy to walk with Shine attached to him that way. "Dutch, were you about to serve dinner? Got room for one more?"

"I always have room for you, Curtis." Dutch slapped her hands together as if everything was settled. She marched back into the kitchen, where I heard her open the cupboard to get out another plate. Dad put a foot on the bottom step, and Larry stepped out of the shadows.

"Elaine's settling into a new life. Don't you think you should ask her if she wants you here?"

Dad flashed a brilliant smile at Larry. I stiffened. This didn't look good. "We've been through a rough time, but we're still married. I think you're the one who's out of place here."

Larry's face turned almost purple. He spluttered for a moment as if his engine was getting warmed up, then took a step towards Dad.

"Stop it! Stop it now!" my mother shouted, leaping between the two men and grabbing Shine. The dogs swirled around them, growling and leaping and biting. Dutch flew out the door, Maureen's frilly apron flapping around her. She brandished a rolling pin of all things.

All this noise and confusion and anger was too much for me. I grabbed Wildfire II, and flew out the open gate. A string of barking dogs nipped at my heels.

Chapter Fifteen
Wild Fire II
July 20

By the time I slowed down, I was dog-free. One by one, the dogs had given up. First, it was the chihuahua and the little dachshund, then the fat lab. The terrier was the last to turn back. I looked at the empty street behind me. Anxiety stabbed at my gut. What would happen to them if they couldn't find their way back to Maureen? I circled back, stopping at the corner to make sure they'd all made it home, then took off again before anybody could see me.

The rainslick roads gleamed in the orange glow of the streetlights, which were just beginning to flicker on. The air smelled of sage and faintly of ozone. Dad once told me that lightning made that scent. Thunder still rolled, like the artillery barrage in *All Quiet on the Western Front.* Nothing was quiet on my front. Especially my heart, that pounded in my chest.

I rode slowly, my legs pushing down on the pedals with a slow determination. Push right. Glide. Push left. Glide. I moved through time and space, not knowing where I was going and not thinking about it. I squeezed the handgrips hard. Tomorrow, perhaps, I would find a police station and hand over Wildfire II. Maybe they'd be able to return it to its rightful owner.

The night darkened until the only light were puddles of orange beneath the streetlights and the headlamps from an occasional passing car. The words *sodium vapor gas-discharge lights* flashed in my head. Was that something Dad taught me, too? It seemed to me that, now that he was here, the lessons he'd taught me came back to me. Why hadn't I remembered them when he was drowning in laundry on the sofa? A bubble of emotion welled up in my chest and threatened to burst out as a sob.

I thought about how much dad had changed since the fire. He'd started so perky, so willing to roll with the punches. But then he'd been beaten down, until there was nothing left of him but an empty shell. I'd felt so alone. So abandoned. Had my mother felt the same way? Is that why she'd turned to this Larry guy for help getting her job, and her life, back into order?

I shook the thought from my head, remembering the words Dutch had used when talking about Paco. Whatever excuses you make for him, whatever problems he's had, he's still made a bad decision. So, I thought, had my mother.

I rode in an arc, planning to return home, but then the violence and noise came back to me and the arc became a full circle. I continued to ride. Slowly. Deliberately. I found myself in the park that Paco had showed me. I didn't even know I could find it again. I left my bike in the tunnel and crawled up into the spot under the bridge. It was dry, and the concrete radiated the day's heat, but I knew that sleeping here was going to be a cold, hard, miserable experience. Spending a night here was better than watching my dad and some sleezy guy in a too tight polo shirt slug it out. I curled into a ball and hoped that morning came quickly. Eventually, I dropped into a kind of half-sleep where the drone of passing cars and my own mental and physical exhaustion made me rise and fall in consciousness, not really awake or asleep.

I jolted awake to the sound of a bomber passing over. It was early dawn and the sky was gray and starless. The Sandia mountains were a dark silhouette against a faint pink glow. It reminded me so strongly of the fire behind the ridge on the day this whole, miserable time began that I smelled smoke. Would I ever see red and orange again and not think of fire, destruction and chaos? The ear that was pressed against the concrete felt like a dead lump on the side of my head. I stretched my stiff, aching joints and hobbled back to Wildfire II, hidden in the darkness of the tunnel.

I rode past several restaurants. None of them had bags of soggy old burgers sitting on the trash cans, although a few had scattered remnants littered on the asphalt. Had some other homeless person beat me to the goodies, or had stray cats ripped the bags to shreds during the night? I was standing on tiptoe, peering into one dumpster when someone in an apron came out the back door of a restaurant. He yelled at me and I jumped on Wildfire II and rode away. The names he called me, and his threat to call the cops rang in my ears, even when I was far enough from him that traffic noise covered his shouts.

The longer I rode, the more my eyes burned. My throat tickled, and the smell of smoke became even more pronounced. But what could be burning in a city where there were no forests to set ablaze? My symptoms had to be the result of a sleepless night and breathing in too much car exhaust. Maybe it was a strange form of PTSD. They say that people who lose an arm continue to feel as if it was there. Maybe my nose smelled smoke whenever I was stressed.

Paco was right. Running away wasn't going to solve my problems. It would just make them worse. I remembered how he'd ridden towards those men on his aunt's porch, ready to face the consequences of his actions. I needed to be as brave as he was. I turned my bike toward home.

The sign with the cow sitting in a basket appeared in front of me. I decided to stop in and see Sal. Maybe she'd give me an old hamburger with a side order of pity and straight talk to bolster me up. I couldn't imagine how much yelling I'd be in for when I got to Maureen's.

Sal stopped outside the door to the kitchen and frowned at Wildfire II. "Hey Doll. Leave that bike outside."

"Can't," I answered. "Paco's got the chain and lock. It'd get stolen."

Sal sighed. "Well, if you have to, you have to. You look like you got run over by a truck. Things not going good?"

I sighed back. "Couldn't get any worse." I leaned my forehead on the table, where it stuck to some dried-up Coke.

"You and Paco didn't spend the night in the bosque? The news says some homeless people started a fire down there."

"It wasn't us," I mumbled into the tabletop.

"Then, where is he?"

Tears welled in my eyes. I sniffed before I answered. "Got in trouble. They took him away."

Sal didn't bother to ask how he got in trouble or who had taken him away. She stood there a moment, tapping her pencil against her order pad. "One Sal special coming up," she said before disappearing into the kitchen.

I turned my head to look at where she had gone. Above the door, the TV soundlessly presented the noon edition of the local news, just like it had last time. The camera focused on a woman with a microphone. Behind her, smoke billowed from what must have been yet another wildfire. She turned and pointed as a bomber lumbered past, dumping a load of orange stuff.

My heart jerked in my chest. Over the reporter's shoulder, I'd spied an adobe stable with blue-painted trim.

I knew that stable.

I leaped to my feet and wheeled Wildfire II towards the door.

Sal backed through the kitchen door, a basket in one hand and a cup in the other. She frowned at me. "Where're you going?"

"Which way to Candelaria?"

Sal's head nodded back the way I had come. I pushed through the door, threw my leg over the center bar, and pushed that bike as hard as I could.

My lungs burned. Not with fire, but with the exertion.

I had never ridden so hard or fast.

Candelaria was all downhill, but I stood on the pedals and pushed anyway.

Right through a red light. I heard the screech of tires. The honks. I didn't look, and I didn't stop.

I reached the place where the sidewalks ended. Police cars blocked the road. I swerved right past those flashing lights and ignored the cops' shouts.

A couple of cars piled high with furniture passed me, going the other way. One honked at me as if trying to warn me to turn around.

I passed the news van and the reporter I had seen on the tv at Sal's place, skidded to a stop, and ran across Mercedes' driveway. Smoke billowed on the other side of the stables. The air was filled with its acrid bitterness, stinging my eyes and making my nose run.

The stable was untouched. I ran inside.

Mercedes' two horses looked at me with white-rimmed eyes. They danced in their stalls, whinnying in terror.

"It's okay! I got you!" I said, trying to exude confidence and calm. Both horses backed into the wall, throwing their heads. I glanced around, grabbed a halter and lead rope off the wall and approached the little paint.

"Okay, Navajo. Let's get this on so I can lead you out of here." I don't know if it was hearing her name, but the little paint bent her head and let me slip the halter on. I strapped it behind her ears, then grabbed another halter and lead rope for the bay.

"Your turn, Galadriel. Let's do this." The bay was having none of it. She threw her head, snorting through nostrils wide with fear. I tried to pat her neck and calm her, but she backed up.

I stood back and wiped my forehead with the back of my hand. The stable air was hot. I could hear the crackle and roar of the fire. If I didn't get these horses out now, it would be too late. I opened the gate on Navajo's stall.

"Git!" I cried. Navajo didn't have to be told twice. She raced from the stall and out onto the road. I watched her go for a second, hoping that someone would catch her and keep her until Mercedes showed up. I turned back and gave Galadirel an authoritative glare.

"Look, girl. You want to go with Navajo? I'm not letting you out until I get this halter on you." I climbed onto the side rail of the stall and reached out the halter. Galadriel was taller than Navajo. She threw her head back, but I managed to slip her nose into the noseband as her head came back down. I climbed onto her back so that I could get the strap behind her ears, then leaned to the side and opened the gate.

For a moment, I thought Galadriel would stay in the stall, paralyzed by her own fear.

Then she bolted.

My head snapped back. I lunged forward, pressing my knees into her sides. Galadriel arced her back and leaped sideways, crashing into the far wall of the stable. I grabbed a handful of mane in the hand that wasn't holding the lead rope and hoped that she would find her way out the door.

She did, but the open space didn't calm her. Galadriel bucked and spun. I felt myself slipping.

And then I felt nothing at all.

Chapter Sixteen
Déjà vu All over Again
July 21

"Punkin. Wake up." My dad's voice called me out of a nightmare. For a moment, I was back in my old bedroom and the fire was just cresting the hill.

I opened my eyes. The room wasn't bathed in an orange glow. It was dark. But even in the dimness I could see Mom and Dad's faces hovering over me, two ghosts or memories of an earlier time.

I closed my eyes again and willed my heart to stop pounding in my ears. This wasn't my room. This wasn't a reliving of the worst day in my life. This was something new and different.

I opened my eyes again and looked past the two dim faces. White curtains hung off a track in the ceiling. Metal railings rimmed the bed. A bag full of water hung over my head. I twitched my arm and watched the tube between it and the bag jerk. Something behind me beeped. I tried to raise my hand. Pain seared through me. It was bandaged like a mummy. My head ached.

"I've got to let Shine know you're ok. She's been worried sick about you." My mother disappeared from my sight. Whatever it was that was behind me beeped again.

"What happened to my hand?" My voice sounded creaky, like a door that hadn't been opened in a long, long time.

"You broke a couple of bones in it," Dad said. "You're going to get a cast when the swelling's down. You even get to pick the color!"

I nodded and looked around again. "Is this *General Hospital*?"

Dad grinned. "That's on TV, Punk. This is real. But yes, it is a hospital. They brought you here yesterday afternoon. In an ambulance. Do you remember?"

I closed my eyes and tried to remember what happened to me. I remembered sleeping under a bridge. Going to Sal's and seeing the fire on the tv. The wild ride. Galadriel refusing to leave her stall. "Mercedes' horses?"

"They're fine, but they wouldn't have survived if you hadn't freed them. The fire burned the stable to the ground. It's out now," Dad said. "Mercedes is how we knew you were in the hospital. Someone saw the fire on the news and called her at the library. She drove home just in time to see medics loading you into an ambulance. The cops had already rounded up the horses, and neighbors had taken them in. Mercedes called Dutch, who called Lainey. We came over as soon as we heard. Mercedes sent these, by the way." My dad held up a huge flower arrangement. It was shaped like a horseshoe, like the kind I'd seen at horseraces.

"Punk! I thought you were dead, like Bilbo! But you're not! You're famous!" Shine leaped onto the foot of my bed. The jolt of her jump ran through me. I thought my head was going to split.

"Shine! Careful with your sister! You know she can't take loud noises or sudden movement," my mother said as she came through the door. Her face hovered over me again, right next to dad's. "Sweetheart, you've got a concussion. We need to keep you still until your poor head has a chance to recover."

"You bruised your brain riding a bucking bronco! And you stayed on a full eight seconds!" Shine shouted, bouncing on the end of the bed as if it were a bronco too. My mother grabbed her and pulled her away.

"And no bright lights, screens, reading, or jumping around, either."

"Got it." I closed my eyes, waiting for the pain to recede. "Shine, what do you mean, I'm famous?"

"You are!" Shine whispers. Even without opening my eyes, I can tell that she's come around and is whispering through the rails on the side of the bed, right near my ear. Her breath is minty fresh. I bet she's eaten all of my mother's Tic Tacs. "That news crew you passed right near Mercedes' house? They caught it all! You racing past! You setting the first horse free! Then riding the other like it was a bucking bronco at the rodeo! It was all on the news last night! How you saved Mercedes' horses! And how you lost Wildfire! They're calling you *The Wildfire Cowgirl*!

"Great," I mutter. I wasn't trying to become a celebrity. I just didn't want to see two horses burn up. And while I'm glad they didn't, I'm not sure right now if it was worth the pain in my head. My hand doesn't feel so great, either.

"But it *is* great," my mother said. "Your story? The UP wire picked it up. It was on *Good Morning America*, and it's gone viral on social media. There are pictures of Wildfire everywhere! Deputy Chavez says that he's done nothing all morning but answer phone calls and emails about Wildfire. Some people say they have leads. Others want to donate money towards a reward to whoever finds him."

The thing behind my bed beeped again.

I opened my eyes in time to see my mother reach over my head. Her hand came back holding a cell phone. "Here. See for yourself."

"What's that?" I croak.

"Lainey, no screens, remember?" Dad said.

"Just for a minute, Curt. It'll do her good." My mother looked right at me. "Punk, we finally got you a new phone. The lady at the store set it up for you, downloaded all your contacts from the cloud. It's been pinging all morning."

The phone had over 7,000 texts, going all the way back to the day of the fire. A good half of them were from Martina or Tiffany. I opened one at random.

"Hey," Tiffany had written, "Been asking at rodeos about Wildfire. I'll keep asking until he's back."

"Saw you on TV!" Martina had texted just this morning. "Went to the website. Printed your poster 10x. Taking them with me when I compete this weekend. Miss U."

The last text posted was from Deputy Chavez. "Lots of leads coming in. I'll contact you when I've sorted through them. Get better soon."

Reading those three texts were enough to make me feel cross-eyed. I closed my eyes and waved my phone about until someone took it from me. "That's great," I said. I laid as still as I could, hoping that everyone would think I'd gone back to sleep.

"Well, aren't you glad you got a phone finally?" my mother asked.

I smiled without opening my eyes. "Thank you," I murmured.

"Let's go get some ice cream from the cafeteria," Shine said in her really loud whisper. I smiled as I heard their footsteps leave the room. It was nice to know that my friends up in Alamitos hadn't forgotten me, after all. And it was nice that Deputy Chavez was finally getting leads. And it was more than nice that my mother and dad were standing next to each other at my bedside. There was hope they'd get together again. But I really needed was to sleep.

Chapter Seventeen
Release and Relief
July 22

The doctor pried my eye wide and shined a little light in it. "She's looking better, Mr. Davis. I think I can release her. Remember the protocol: No strenuous activity or sports until her doctor's cleared her, only acetaminophen and ice packs for headaches, no screens, reading, or heavy thinking, lots of rest, preferably in a cool, dark, quiet room, and keep the diet light for awhile to protect against nausea."

"Got it," my dad answered, "and I'll be sure to call our family practitioner if she experiences double vision or nose bleeds."

"Watch for personality changes, unusual drowsiness, and numbness in the face, too."

My dad grinned. "She's a teenage girl. Personality swings are normal."

The doctor smiled back. He slapped his hands against his thighs and walked towards the door. "I'll let you be the judge of that. I'll tell the nurse to come in and unhook your IVs so you can change into clothes while I work up the release papers." He stopped in the doorway, turned, and winked at me. "And no riding bucking broncos for awhile!"

Once he was gone, I looked over at my dad, who was texting someone on his phone. "I'll be glad to get out of here. Everyone's been super nice and all, but I want to go home."

Dad's hand stopped typing. "That's something we need to talk about. Where you're going. Your mother isn't sure what she wants to do just yet. She'll be staying on with Maureen, at least until she decides whether she wants to get an apartment here in town or come back to Alamitos." My throat went dry.

"But there's hope, Punkin. Your mother will be coming up once a week so she and I can talk with a counselor together. The same counselor I'm seeing on my own right now." He picked up the little kit with toothpaste and such and put it into the bed pan I hadn't used.

The nurse came in, so dad and I stopped talking. She buzzed around the bed, lowering guardrails, turning things off, and pulling needles out of my arm. She slapped a piece of gauze on the bruised place where the needle had been, wrapped it with purple tape, gathered up all her supplies, then scurried out the door.

"Is this about that Larry guy?"

Dad sat down in the chair. "Nope. He's out of the picture. Right after you left, your mother told Larry to take a hike, and he started yelling about how she owed him, his bringing her stuff down from the lab and all that. She decided he wasn't the hero she'd made him out to be. I hear he's applied for a transfer to either the California or Tennessee facilities."

"But if he's gone, why . . . .?"

Dad put up a hand to stop me from finishing the question. "Larry was only part of the problem, Punk. Your mom and I have a lot we need to work through before we get back together. A lot to decide. So, for the time being, you'll have some decisions of your own to make. Do you want to come home to the white tin can so you can go to school in Alamitos? Or stay here with Maureen and Dutch and go to the high school here? It's your decision to make, only school starts in three weeks, and if you're staying here, your mom has to get you registered."

I closed my eyes, fighting to keep in the tears that wanted to roll down my face. "Don't make me choose between you."

"We're not," Dad said. "The only decision right now should be where you go to school."

I nodded. "Does Shine get to choose, too?"

"She already has. Zoos, museums and ice cream parlors won. Not surprised. Dutch and Maureen have been treating her like a princess."

An aide arrived with a wheelchair. Dad waved her off. "Thanks, but we're not quite ready to leave yet. I can wheel her out when we're ready."

I raised my eyebrows. "What are we waiting for?"

"Me," Mercedes entered the room, lifting up a shopping bag. "Hello, there! I'm Mercedes Escudero, stylist to the stars. I've brought you some new clothes.

"I think that's my cue to go get a cup of coffee from the cafeteria. I'll be back in, what? Half an hour?"

Mercedes nodded. "That should do it." She turned back and smiled at me. "There's a news crew waiting by the front door. Your mom and I want you to look good for them. Here." She pulled out a new pair of jeans and a black velvet shirt and held them out to me.

"But it's summer," I said.

"So? Roll up the sleeves. You're going to love how soft and silky it feels against your skin."

Mercedes reached into the bag and pulled out my old boots, but they'd been cleaned and polished so well that I hardly recognized them. She reached back in and pulled out a belt. I stared at the buckle and nearly choked on happy tears.

"You found my buckle!"

Mercedes shook her head. "Not the real one. A replacement. Deputy Chavez' cousin, your friend Martina described it to me. I talked with the rodeo organizers, and they were able to help. We librarians know how to do these things." She tilted her head and looked me up and down. "Yep. You look like what the newscasters expect the Wildfire Cowgirl to look like. Now, let's brush your hair until it's burnished copper, give you a slick of lipstick, and polish those nails. I promise you, it'll be easier to face the cameras that way. It's amazing how nail polish brings out the tigress in us women."

I was still waving my hands in the air, trying to dry my nails when my Dad came back with the wheelchair aide.

"Wow," Dad said. "It's as if my little Punkin grew up while I was getting a cup of coffee."

"If a summer like she's had doesn't age her, nothing will," Mercedes said, then smiled. "I think your little Punkin has been on the way out a long time. Time to meet your daughter, the mature young woman named Margaret."

"Margaret, your chariot awaits," Dad said, sweeping his hand toward the wheelchair.

"I can walk," I said.

The aide shook her head. "Hospital policy." As soon as I was seated, Dad piled my bag of toiletries and a couple of the flower arrangements on my lap. I held up my hand.

"I'll take the horseshoe flowers. Can you give the rest to other patients? The ones that don't have any? I'd rather share than have them go all wilty in the car."

"That's nice of you," the aide said. "Just what I'd expect from a selfless hero."

I clamped my lips tightly together so I wouldn't argue with her. People'd gotten the wrong idea since my story hit the news. Heroes decide to do good things, to sacrifice for others. I hadn't even thought about it before I'd gotten Mercedes' horses out of the stable. I was no hero. Just an impulsive kid.

We rolled out the hospital's big double doors and into a crowd of waiting cameras. The aide and Mercedes stood with me and helped me answer questions while dad sprinted across the parking lot, then returned in his old pick up.

"Keep in touch! We're all proud of you!" the aide said as she placed my flowers on my lap and slammed the pickup door. I waved at Mercedes, the aide, and the cameras as the pickup rumbled away.

Dad handed me his sunglasses. "We need to get a pair for you. To keep that sun from cooking your brain."

I laughed. "Let's swing by the drug store and pick some up. While we're there, I'd like to get something for a friend. Then, can we stop by Maureen's on our way out of town?"

"We're having dinner there. Already planned."

I leaned back and closed my eyes. I had a lot to think about, but the doctor had told me not to think too much, which was good because my thoughts just weren't organizing themselves. But I had a few plans and, I thought, enough brain cells left to manage them.

Chapter Eighteen
Homecoming
July 22

Shine ran out and opened the gate when Dad pulled up in front of Maureen and Dutch's house. The dogs swirled around us, panting and whining and demanding that I pat each one of them. Maureen and my mother stood on the porch, smiling like I was a long lost relative or something.

"Well, look at you! Welcome back!" Dutch said. "Dinner's not for a couple hours yet. Why don't you go lie down? I'll get a cold compress for your eyes."

I stepped onto the porch and gave both her and mom a one-armed hug. "Leave it to a nurse to know what's good for me. But I've got a little something I gotta do first, okay?"

Dutch scowled. "Does it involve running, bikes, or bronco busting?"

"Nope. Promise," I lifted the shopping bag, as if that explained what I had planned. Dutch's face softened into a grin. She held the door for me, the others, and the dog parade.

I went into the dinning room, where I snatched a *Get Out of Jail Free* card off the table, then I rifled through the drawer in the china hutch until I found a pen and a roll of tape. I taped the card to the last page of the cross sums book that dad had bought for me at the drug store, then I turned to the front page, where I wrote

This isn't the same as solitaire online, and it won't do any better at solving your problems, but I hope it'll help you pass the time. Maybe it'll help you with your math, too. Ha ha. I miss you! Hope to see you soon. Your friend, Chica

I dug around in the drawer some more until I found a pair of old scissors, then I pulled one of the paper grocery bags from the stack that was tucked between the china hutch and the wall. I cut open the bag and used it to wrap up the book. I dug in the drawer some more, found a sharpie, and wrote my Alamito address in the upper left corner as if it were a package to be mailed.

"Be back in a minute!" I yelled as I went out the door. I got out fast enough that not even one dog followed me.

Lluvia blinked and her eyebrows flew up when she opened the front door. "Chica? Paco's not here."

"I know." I handed the package over to her. "I wanted him to have this. Can you take it to him? Or mail it?"

Lluvia's eyes filled with tears. "Si, Chica. I visit him on Saturdays. But I can mail it, if you want it there faster."

"Either way. Whatever works for you is fine," I said. Really, I had no idea how long it was until Saturday. I'd completely lost track of the days. I pointed at my return address. "There's no house there right now. Just a burned lot. But the post office keeps my mail so I can go in and pick it up. I hope he'll write."

Lluvia smiled. "I hope so, too. You were a good friend." She slid the door closed and I went back and took my Dutch-mandated nap.

I didn't wake until Shine came in and shook me. "Punk! You can sleep through anything! Didn't you hear us all?"

"I didn't hear anything," I said with a groan. I wiped the drool from the side of my face. My head felt like it was stuffed with felt. I rolled onto my side and got up, then followed Shine into a kitchen that was filled with people. My dad and mom, Maureen and Dutch, Shine and Mercedes all looked up and smiled at me.

"Home comes the conquering hero!" Mercedes gave me a thumbs up. I felt my face go red.

"Everybody, stop looking at me. I'm no hero. Where'd you get that line, anyway?" I muttered as Dad helped me into a seat.

"I don't know, actually. Back when I was in high school, it's what my dad used to say whenever I came home from getting some award at school," Mercedes said. "And you might not think you're a hero, but I will be forever grateful to you for saving Galadriel and Navajo. Promise me you'll never risk your life for an animal again, though. You are more precious than even my equine babies."

"Precious to all of us," Maureen said as she began to bring bowls and platters to the table. "Here ya go, Precious. Chicken fried steak, with mashed potatoes and plenty of cream gravy. Don't go dribbling it on that pretty new shirt of yours."

"I propose a toast!" Dad lifted his glass of milk. The rest of us followed his lead. "To the precious among us, and to the brave! To Punk, and to Maureen and Dutch! Congratulations!" Everyone murmured the names as we clinked our milk glasses and took sips.

I looked at Maureen, who was smiling at me in a rather conspiratorial way. "While you were in the hospital, Dutch and I decided to get married. It's been a long time coming, but the world has changed and we're ready to change with it."

"You are? That's great!" I said. Marriage or no marriage, Maureen and Dutch were just Maureen and Dutch to me. They deserved to be happy.

"Mercedes is going to stand up with us. Who needs a best man when we've got a woman like her!" Dutch said.

"And I'll be the matron of honor," my mom said.

"And I'm going to be the flower girl!" Shine toasted so hard that milk sloshed down her upraised arm.

"It's going to be nothing fancy," Dutch said. "We'll do it here at the house, so the dogs and cats can be our witnesses. We're thinking we'll do it during the Balloon Fiesta. Then, maybe, we can entice some old friends to come."

"I think it's wonderful!" I got out of my seat and hugged them both. I noticed that my mother was smiling at dad. Perhaps there was hope for the two of them, too.

"So, have you decided where you're going to school this fall? Mom asked when I'd gotten back into my seat.

I felt my forehead wrinkle as I shrugged. "I don't know. I like it here, love you and Maureen and Dutch. And leaving Shine would be hard. But all my friends are in Alamitos. And Deputy Chavez is there, too. I want to check in with him. Now that I've gotten all this publicity, maybe something will happen."

Mom pushed her lips together and gave a satisfied nod. "You've still got some time to think about it. Go up with your dad. Check in with your friends and that sheriff's deputy. Then, if you like, stay there. After all, your first year at high school is going to be much easier if you're with your friends."

"You and Dad can come visit me some weekends," Shine said. "I'll even let you sleep in my room! And I can come sometimes and visit you, too."

"And you'll come down for the wedding," Maureen said.

I nodded my head so hard I felt my brain smacking my skull. "Oh, I wouldn't miss that for the world."

After dinner, dad helped me pack my things and we began the drive back to Alamitos. The green reflection of the dashboard on my window reminded me of the trip down the mountain, when Mom had first taken us to see Maureen and Dutch. "I remember making some wishes when Mom took us away," I said. "I wanted to find Wildfire. I wanted you to get off the couch and start planning again. I wanted our building permit to be approved. And I wanted life to get back to normal."

"Some of that's happened," Dad said. "I've got my old job back, doing maintenance at the lab. It'll keep me busy until Shine comes back, if she comes back. Truth is, you don't need me home all the time anymore. And I've got house plans started. But I'm still waiting on permitting. And who knows? All the news stories might help you get Wildfire back. But Punk, I'm not sure we'll ever get back to normal again. At least, not the way it used to be."

"So, it's back to the white tin can, huh?"

Dad nodded. "At least for the time being."

"But it's only temporary."

"You bet, Punk. All of it is only temporary, and we manage to do the best we can." The car turned off the flats and began following a long line of red tail lights up the winding mountain road to Alamito. I brushed back a tear that had slipped from my eye. I was tired of the temporary. I wanted to find one place to rebuild my life, where I'll stay for a long, long time.

Chapter Nineteen
The Call
July 23rd

Sheila, the friendly waitress who'd let me hang around Jack's Flapjack House all summer looked up as I walked in the door. "Hey! It's our local celebrity, the Wildfire Cowgirl! Welcome back! Anything you want is on the house."

"I'm meeting a couple of friends here," I said as I looked over her shoulder.

Sheila smiled. "I think they're in the back. They thought you'd want a quiet booth." I heard a couple of shrieks and Tiffany and Martina rushed down the aisle waving their arms like crazed rock band groupies. We hugged and kissed and made a scene that got the attention of everyone in the place before Tiffany and Martina dragged me back to the big round booth in the corner. I slid in and relaxed. Now that the monsoons had come, there were no bombers to count. I did not miss their drone.

"It's so good to be back," I said. "Everything looks so green."

Martina shook her head. "Except where the fire swept through. That's all as bare as the moon."

"With blackened poles that used to be trees," Tiffany added. "The forest service is cutting them down. They're a hazard: might fall on some hiker or something."

Martina nodded. "And the monsoons are causing a lot of soil run off in the burn areas. The flash floods in the arroyos look like chocolate milk shakes."

I nodded. "My dad says he and I are going to rent a bobcat and build some retaining walls on the edges of our building site."

"A bobcat? Cool! Can I come drive it?" Tiffany asked. Before I answered, my cell phone rang. It was Deputy Chavez. Sheila the waitress came by, pad in hand to take our order. I pointed to the phone and waved my hand. She nodded and went away.

"Are you sitting down?" Deputy Chavez asked when I answered.

"Yes," I said. My voice was steady and calm, but my heart wasn't. It pounded, and my knee bounced up and down. Ever since I left a message yesterday telling him I was back, I'd been hoping he'd call with good news.

"I think I've found Wildfire."

"Really?" I said, my voice steady. Tiffany and Martina tilted their heads. looking like two puppies as they tried to understand the conversation just from my side of it.

"Really! A man who owns a riding stable in Amarillo, Texas was watching the news when it aired a human-interest story on *The Wildfire Cowgirl.* He called his local sheriff, who called me. He bought a horse in an auction on May 2nd· And he thinks it's Wildfire. He sent me a picture. It sure looks like him. But none of the paperwork matches."

"Could the paperwork be forged?" I asked. Tiffany and Martina's heads tilted the other direction.

"That's what I'm thinking, amiga." Deputy Chavez' voice was so bubbly I swear he was popping buttons off his shirt. I sucked in a big breath. This was too good to be true.

"So, what do we do now?" Tiffany and Martina started bobbing up and down. Their mouths were stretched out sideways in expectant grimaces.

"Come in and look at the picture," he said. "Verify that I'm right. Can you come in this afternoon?"

"I'm on my way now. Be there in fifteen minutes." I ended the call and looked at Tiffany and Martina, who were staring at me, wide eyed, their mouths hanging open. "Deputy Chavez thinks he's found Wildfire."

My friends pumped the air with their fists, whooping and cheering so loud that Sheila rushed over to find out what was going on.

"The sheriff's found Wildfire!" Tiffany shrieked. Everyone in Jack's Flapjack House stood up and clapped. I burst into tears.

"At least, he hopes so," I said. "I'm going to his office now, to see." I had to walk through a crowd of people who all wanted to slap my back or shake my hand. Finally, Martina got in front of me and elbowed a way through the crowd. The three of us walked the two blocks to the Sherriff's office, where I found Ernesto Chavez staring out the front door. He broke into a big smile as he opened the door and let us in.

"I see you've got your posse with you. Hey there, Martina."

"And I'm Tiffany. Thanks for helping Punk, I mean Margaret." Tiffany held out her hand and she and Deputy Chavez shook before he escorted us into his office. The desk was strewn with printed out emails, many of which had pictures of horses. My eyes scanned them all. I hadn't realized just how many bays were out there.

"This is it," Deputy Chavez said, "What do you think?" He picked up a paper and handed it to me. I heard Tiffany and Martina both suck in their breaths. They hovered just behind me, peering over my shoulder.

I shook my head. "This isn't him."

I heard both Tiffany and Martina groan.

"But this one? I think this is." I picked up another paper and studied the picture. Hard. My heart pounded so loud it made my ears want to pop. Deputy Chavez took the paper from my hand and studied it.

"This is from a woman who owns a riding stable in Macon, Georgia. She saw *The Wildfire Cowgirl* on TV, too. She bought this horse in an auction on May 9th. None of her paperwork matches, either."

"But, I really think it's him," I said.

Deputy Chavez' mouth screwed up sideways. "They look the same to me. How can you be so sure this one's it and the other isn't?"

Martina gave out a big harrumph. "It's her horse! She'd know him anywhere."

"Okay, then," Deputy Chavez said. "We drive to Macon, Georgia and see for ourselves. If it really is Wildfire, we bring him back with us."

"I don't have a horse trailer," I said. My mind raced with a hundred different questions. Tiffany started whispering behind me, I'm guessing she was asking Martina if her parents would let me borrow their trailer.

"You may not, but the Sherriff does. And this is official business. I'd like you there to identify Wildfire. Think your father can accompany us?" Deputy Chavez asked.

"I think so. Let me give him a call. When will we leave?"

"As soon as possible. And the more documents we have, the better. Bills of sale. Coggins Papers. Vet Records. Pictures of you and Wildfire. They can all help bolster your case."

I called Dad, who left work to talk with Deputy Chavez while Tiffany, Martina and I stood outside and made the receptionist nervous. When Dad was done talking, he gave Tiffany and Martina rides home.

"I can't go with you, Punk," Dad said as we drove back to the white tin can. "I've got too much to do before Wildfire gets here. But I called your mom. She's taking time off to go with you."

"My mother? Taking time off?" I asked.

Dad nodded. "She'd got over six months of leave racked up. Decided this was as good a reason as any to take some of it. She'll be up here tomorrow."

"It might not even be Wildfire," I said, cautiously preparing my heart for disappointment. "Georgia is a long way from here. It could be some other bay."

"True," dad said. "You won't know until you see him."

I thought about that all the way to Georgia. My mother rode in the front seat with Deputy Chavez while I slumped in the back, staring out at the blur going past the window without focusing on any of it. Would I even recognize Wildfire when I saw him. Had I forgotten what he looked like? The special way he threw his head and snorted when he saw me? The smell that was Wildfire's alone? And would he remember me? What if we stared at each other and neither of us reacted? Would I walk away from Wildfire without even knowing it? I kept telling myself that it was likely that this horse wasn't Wildfire, and that I shouldn't be disappointed, but the farther we traveled, the more dread and anticipation built up in my heart, two warring emotions tearing me apart.

"We're here, amigos." Deputy Chavez pulled off the road, past a sign that read *Pleasant Pines Horseback Riding and Stables.* He parked next to a white Ford Explorer that had *Sherriff Bibb Country* written on its side. In front of it stood a white, clapboard house with a large porch that had a sign that read 'OFFICE' hung from it. Behind the office, ponies carried riding-helmeted girls as they bounced around in a circle inside a metal-roofed riding arena. Behind them, dovecotes topped white stables. Everything looked so clean and neat. I opened the door and the warm, moist air smelled of pine trees and horses.

A man and a woman came out of the office as we approached it. The man wore a black uniform and a hat that looked like Smokey Bear's hat, so different from Deputy Chavez's khakis and Stetson that I wouldn't have recognized him as a Sheriff's Deputy. The woman wore a red jacket and tall black boots. She looked like she had been posing for one of those paintings of a fox hunt in England.

"Miz Davis? Deputy Chavez? Miss? I'm Deputy David Cooke, Bibb County Sheriff's Department. And this is Ms. Arabella Fino, the owner of Pleasant Pines."

Ms. Fino inclined her head. "So good of you to drive all this way. I hope this won't be a disappointment to you. Shall we?" She gestured towards the stables. I followed along, my heart pounding so hard it was difficult to hear what Ms. Fino said.

"Trigger Happy is a magnificent horse: intelligent and gentle. But I knew soon after I bought him that he wasn't whom he was purported to be. For one thing, he is very uncomfortable being ridden English."

"He's always been Western," my mother said.

Ms. Fino turned and nodded. "That much became evident quite quickly. And while that is not bad, it is not what I had been led to believe. And another thing: we here at Pleasant Pines take our horses' health very seriously. You are, I assume, familiar with Coggins tests?"

My mother turned to me, a perplexed look wrinkling her brow. She really knew nothing about horses. "Of course," I said. "Our veterinarian does one every year."

Ms. Fino smiled. "So you know that it's a blood sample that detects an antibody that a horse has if it's had the Equine Infectious Anemia virus. Well, the papers that came with Trigger Happy said that he'd had EIA in the past. But just to protect our animals, we quarantine newcomers until our veterinarian can look them over. He did a blood draw, and one of the things he found was a negative result for the EIA Antibody."

"That's right! Wildfire's never had EIA!" I fumbled through the manila folder until I found Wildfire's Coggins Papers. In addition to his antibody result, the papers have all kinds of information about me, my vet, and Wildfire. There are even pictures of him taken from the side and a front view of his head. I handed the Coggins paper to Ms. Fino, who studied it before handing it to Deputy Cooke.

"I have more papers!" I said. "Bill of sale! Veterinarian records! Ribbons he's won at rodeos and at the county fair!"

Ms. Fino waved her hand dismissively and continued towards the stable. "Clearly, Trigger Happy is not who his papers claim he is. The question remains, is he Wildfire? Let's see what he says when he sees you."

We passed the stables, which were filled with horses. Their heads turned as they watched us pass by. Behind the stables was a smaller building with only a couple of stalls.

"Wildfire?" I called. Almost instantly a bay head stuck over the gate. He threw his head once, twice, three times and snorted, then pressed his chest into the gate, straining to get near me. I ran up to him and threw my arms around his neck, bursting into tears. Wildfire nuzzled the top of my head. He threw his head over my shoulder and drew me in close.

"Well," Deputy Cooke said, "I think that answers that."

"Indeed," Ms. Fino said. "So, tell me, what should be our next course of action?"

"We let these good people get on the road home," he said. "Then we start looking for the person who sold you this horse."

Chapter Twenty
Homecoming
August 8

I woke up as Deputy Chavez's tires bumped into the concrete parking stop. We were in the parking lot of Jack's Flapjack House. I groaned and brushed the hair out of my eyes. "Don't stop now! We're almost home!"

My mother pointed at the sign, which read *Welcome Home WF & WFCG.*

"WF? CG?" I asked.

Mom smiled back at me. "Wildfire and Wildfire Cow Girl. Sorry, Punk, but you've got some friends, fans and supporters to thank."

"Being a celebrity can be soooo trying," Deputy Chavez said with a laugh.

I reached over the seat and laid a hand on my mother's shoulder. "Before we go in there, I want to thank you, Mom, for taking time off and going with me to Georgia. It meant a lot to me."

My mother turned her head. Her eyes glistened as she laid a hand on my hand. It was trembling. "Do you realize that's the first time you've called me Mom instead of Mother in a long, long time?"

"Are you two going to go in, or do I have to drag you?" Deputy Chavez asked. He held the door for me while I stepped into a standing-room only crowd of cheering people. Everyone was there! My dad and sister, Tiffany, Martina, my friend Julia who used to live up at the end of our street, and a dozen or so other school friends, Mr. Chen, a lot of my old teachers, even the lady who sat at the front table in the shelter! They all crowded around, slapping my back and shouting at me, telling me about how they saw my picture on the news, or what they remembered from the night of the fire, or how much they loved their dog. It was bewildering and loud, and a lot of it didn't make any sense to me, so I just kept shaking hands and thanking people.

Sheila, the nice waitress, elbowed her way through the crowd. She turned her back to me and started banging on a glass with a spoon until everyone grew quiet. "We're all so happy to see Wildfire and the Wildfire Cowgirl reunited," she said before the crowd began cheering and she had to bang on the glass again to get their attention. "It's been a long and difficult road home, Margaret, and we're all proud of the grit you've shown. We at Jack's Flapjack House wanted you to know that you weren't alone on that road. We put together a little campaign for funds to pay for the expenses you've incurred. You are our hero!"

Again, the crowd started cheering as a huge check got passed, hand to hand, from the kitchen. Sheila turned to me and yelled over the cheers. "Last time you were here, I said anything you wanted was on the house. But you left before ordering, so the offer still stands."

I hugged her, partly out of gratitude and partly so she could hear me in the crowd. "Thank you! But what I really want right now is to get Wildfire home. Can I take a raincheck?"

Sheila smiled. "You bet!"

Mom and I elbowed our way over to Shine and Dad, who grinned through the stubble of his new beard. Shine shouted to anyone who looked her way that she was my sister.

"We got him! You found a place to board him?" I asked.

Dad grinned at Mom. "Time to show her?"

"Time," Mom said. "I think these people have taken enough of her time. Go ahead and take her with you. I'll ride with Deputy Chavez."

We made our way to the door, shaking hands and saying thanks all the way. I was glad they didn't expect me to make a speech. Dad and I climbed into his old, beat up truck and the rumbling engine hid all the outside noises.

"I'm so glad you're back," Dad said. "I've missed you."

I nodded. "It took a lot longer than I thought it would. Lots of papers to fill out, and a lot of deputies and agents who wanted to hear all about Trudy Goodheart and the Equine Assistance Agency. All of the papers that called Wildfire Trigger Happy were forged. The person who sold Wildfire at the auction where Ms. Fino bought him had a fake name, too. It's not going to be easy to track down the other three horses Goodheart stole."

"But now there's hope. The trail isn't as cold as it had been," Dad said.

"Yup," I added. "And everyone's been so nice. Ms. Fino kept Wildfire for us, and the local branch of Future Farmers of America paid for two motel rooms, one for me and mom and the other for Deputy Chavez. Even though he said he was on official business and could get reimbursed!"

"Good people." Dad turned the car onto Ridgecrest Drive, the street that our house used to be on.

"Did you find a stable close to our old house?" The words stuck in my throat. Thc street looked so desolate. I remember when it was thick with pine trees and scrubby oaks.

"Nope," Dad said. "But I built one while you were gone. He pulled into what had been our driveway. Two new structures stood amidst piles of dirt: a stable, and a tiny little house that looked like an overgrown playhouse. I jumped out of the car and raced to the stable.

Dad rapped his knuckles against the wall and it mades a sound like Paco's garage door. "It's metal. Going to be awfully noisy in a hailstorm, but it was the quickest thing to put up, and I wanted it in place when Wildfire got back. I bought some water and feed buckets, some curry combs and hoof pickers, and a manure fork and wheelbarrow, but we'll need to buy you a new saddle and some other tack. But at least he's got a place to call home. Now, come see this."

I followed him to the little house. Dad opened the door and stepped aside to let me through. Inside were a set of bunkbeds, a table by the window, and a tiny kitchen counter, with a sink, a coffee maker and a microwave. I opened the little fridge under the counter and found it stocked with yogurts, berries, juice and milk. A cupboard above the counter held a few dishes and a few microwavable, shelf stable meals.

I heard tires on the gravel and raced outside to see Deputy Chavez pulling in with the horse trailer.

"Well, well! Looks like you've been busy," Mom said as I began walking Wildfire down the ramp.

"It's going to be a little tight, but Punk and I can stay here until we get a real house built," Dad said. I've talked with the Big Brass, and they've agreed to let me work nights. That way, I can be here for Wildfire during the day, while Punk's at school."

He pointed to a big plastic barrel attached to the side of the house. "We've got electric lights and a little heater, but no water yet. I fill that barrel every night. It feeds down to the sink inside. Waste water comes out that pipe there and just soaks into the ground. There's a privy out back. Punk and I will have to go down to the white tin can to take our showers, or if we want to cook anything fancier than a microwave meal. When the house is built, this can become a playhouse for Shine, or I can add on a bathroom and it'll be a guesthouse."

"Or a home office for me?" Mom asked.

Dad grinned from ear to ear. "That could happen."

I led Wildfire into the stable. Although he'd never been in this building before, his easy breath and the way his tail swung loose and relaxed seemed to tell me that he knew this was home. I hung up his halter, then sat down in the straw and leaned my head against the wall. It was over. After months of frustration and fear, I'd recovered my horse and was home at last. Wildfire bent his neck and nuzzled the top of my head, making little nickering noises.

"Welp," said Deputy Chavez, "I guess it's time for me to mosey into the sunset."

"Thank you for all your help." Too exhausted to get up, I waved one hand at him.

"Just doing my job." He touched the brim of his Stetson and walked back to his truck.

Dad stuck his head in the door. "I'm going to drive your mom back to the white tin can so she can pick up her car and get back to Maureen's. Don't be surprised if it takes me a while to get back. We may just sit and talk for a while.

I nodded. "You do that. Me and Wildfire can keep each other company just fine."

"Oh, and this came for you." Dad handed me an envelope. The return address let me know it was from Paco. Before I'd stuck my finger under the flap, I heard dad's old pick-up rumbling down the driveway.

Dear Chica,

Thank you for the whole book of cross sums. I hate them and they make my head hurt, but I guess if I can't play solitaire, they're the next best thing. Who knows? Maybe I'll learn some math. Do you think the get-out-of-jail-card will really work?

The D Home isn't so bad as long as I keep my head down and don't get any of the really hard dudes mad. My social worker says I'm going to graduate on time. And I get fed and got a warm bed. I miss Lluvia's and I miss going for bike rides. I'm not working on bikes no more, and I won't. Not ever. I think maybe it's time to learn a different trade.

My social worker says if I keep out of trouble, they might find a foster family for me. He thinks maybe someone far away from all the bad influences in my life here in town. Know any nice families in Alamitos that need a hard-working dude who wants to learn the construction trade? Like, someone rebuilding a house?

Bueno bye, your friend, Paco.

Smiling, I refolded the letter and stuck it back in the envelope. I leaned my head against the stable wall and closed my eyes, happy to drift off to sleep with the smell of Wildfire filling my nostrils.

About The Author

A native New Mexican, Jennifer Bohnhoff spent two decades teaching Language Arts and History to middle school and high school students. She now writes for middle school through adult readers and loves speaking in classrooms and to adult groups about the history behind her novels.

Mrs. Bohnhoff lives in the mountains of central New Mexico with her husband and a rottweiler named Panzer.

Other books by Jennifer Bohnhoff

Where Duty Calls
Book 1 of Rebels Along the Rio Grande

Texan Jemmy Martin and New Mexican Raul Atencio don't want to be involved in the Civil War that's splitting the United States, but at a small crossing of the Rio Grande they become embroiled in a battle that could change the destiny of two nations.

FREE Teacher's Guide! Over 100 pages of discussion questions, activities, worksheets and quizzes all tied to the common core standards.

Book 2, The Worst Enemy, is due out August 2023.

The Anderson Chronicles

Hector Anderson is a geeky middle school boy who loves his wacky family, even if they embarrass him. The funny, short contemporary novels are perfect for both boys and girls in grades 4-6 who are feeling awkward about growing up and being themselves. Join Hec, Calvin, Stevie, Chloe and their parents as they learn about life, love, and being the best they can be.

In **Tweet Sarts**, Valentine's Day is coming, and while love is in the air, no one knows exactly what to do with it.

In **Jingle Night**, the holidays are coming. Hec wants to buy gifts for his family, but a lot of things are ruining the holiday spirit.

In **Super Hec**, Mom decides that spring is the perfect time for the family to get in shape. Will training for a 5K make Hec able to leap over bullies in a single bound?

A Blaze of Poppies

Feisty little Agnes Day is determined to keep the family ranch and run it alone on her own terms. A family death along with the attack of a nearby town threatens her ability to keep the ranch—making her goal seemingly impossible. Agnes presses on and trains to become a nurse, then volunteers to go over there to help the thousands of doughboys suffering in the trenches of the greatest war the world has known.

Can Agnes secure a peaceful future on the Sunrise Ranch after the insanity and bloodshed of war? Dare she hope to share that future with someone else?

The Last Song of the Swan

A dual timeline novel about prejudice and cultural exclusion

What if Beowulf is the written account of a story that stretches back to the dawn of time? Helen Bowie asks this question. Hrunting, daughter of Unferth, the mage of Heorot, lives it. Both women fight for the rights of social outsiders against powerful men, heroes with the power to change society, perhaps for the better, perhaps not. The stories of two women who lived 25,000 years apart asks the reader to consider who determines who is human and who must be destroyed.

Code: Elephants on the Moon

A novel about a French resistance fighter in Normandy during World War II is written for middle grade and older readers.

As D-Day looms ever closer, a girl in a small town in Normandy joins the Resistance, where she learns some dark family secrets that allow her to follow her own conscience and to understand the coded messages on the radio.

On Fledgling Wings

Nathaniel Marshal is a bully with a short temper and an empty place in his heart left by the mother who disappeared when he was a baby. The spoiled boy can't wait to leave boring Staywell and begin training so he can become a knight like his father, the cold and distant Sir Amren. But when he arrives at Farleigh, he finds himself in a place of death and danger.

The Bent Reed

It's June of 1863 and Sarah McCoombs feels isolated and uncomfortable when her mother pulls her from school and allows a doctor to treat her scoliosis with a cumbersome body cast. She thinks life can't get much worse, but she's wrong. When the McCoombs farm becomes a battle field and then a hospital, Sarah must reach deep inside herself to find the strength to cope as she nurses wounded soldiers from both sides. Can she find even more courage to continue to follow her dreams despite her physical disabilities and her disapproving mother?

Made in the USA
Middletown, DE
07 May 2023

29810253R00076